AFTERGLOW

AFTERGLOW

✦✦✦✦

More
stories of
lesbian desire

Karen Barber, editor

Boston ✦ Lace Publications
an imprint of Alyson Publications, Inc.

Copyright © 1993 by Alyson Publications, Inc.
Cover art copyright © 1993 by Catherine Hopkins.
All rights reserved.

Typeset and printed in the United States of America.

This is a paperback original from Lace Publications,
an imprint of Alyson Publications, Inc.,
40 Plympton St., Boston, Mass. 02118.
Distributed in England by GMP Publishers,
P.O. Box 247, London N17 9QR, England.

This book is printed on acid-free, recycled paper.

First edition: July 1993

5 4 3 2 1

ISBN 1-55583-315-2

"Innocent Lust" appeared in slightly different form in *Piece of My Heart:
A Lesbian of Colour Anthology,* copyright © 1991 by Sister Vision Press.
Reprinted with permission of the author.

◆ *For Susan,*
you will always be my pumpkin, regardless

Contents

◆◆◆◆

Introduction

✦✦✦✦

I'm excited to be offering lesbians a follow-up to *Bush-fire: Stories of lesbian desire*. I was thrilled with the warm response the first book received; I hope this collection is greeted with the same enthusiasm. The authors have done a fabulous job capturing the diversity of the lesbian sexual experience. And as you'll see in these stories, while desire can be painful, it is a feeling to be treasured. Enjoy!

I would like to thank the women who made this book possible. First and foremost, my sister Leslie, who, with little reward, assisted me with the editing of these stories. I'd also like to thank all seventeen contributors who were brave enough to write about sex for all the world to see; Tina Portillo for meticulously proofreading the book; Susan Reddy and Kiki Zeldes for reading manuscripts and offering opinions and criticisms; and Catherine Hopkins for producing a beautiful and sexy cover. And finally I would like to thank Lynne Yamaguchi Fletcher for teaching me a thing or two about editing, as well as a thing or two about myself. These past months haven't been easy, but they've certainly been worth it. Thank you all.

—*Karen Barber*

What is the goal & how will we know when we get there?

◆◆◆◆   *Jean Swallow*

September, 1992

Dear BW:
   Okay, I admit it. Not taking the phone number for where you'd be this weekend was stupid. Defiant. Defended. And if it hurt you or made you think I wasn't interested in where you'd be, well, I guess I got what I deserved. It's two in the morning, I'm still awake, and I'm not having a good time. I know better than to behave like this. Or I ought to by now.

   Naturally, it did not occur to me until about ten minutes after you had left home on Friday, when it was no longer possible to get hold of you, that I might be making a mistake in not getting the number. By the time you get home tomorrow you may not have any more room on your answering machine, because I will have used it all, and for useless sentimental drivel, and I'm sorry. I am quite aware this is not age-appropriate behavior for a gainfully employed, stable, and secure lesbian who just turned forty, but it seems I've failed to plan for a single, simple factor: infatuation, the great leveler. I feel like I've been hit by a truck, and I know I'm behaving like it. I apologize. I hate this. I feel like a teenager, all hormones. Don't get me started.

Not that you have to do much anymore, not that either of us has to do much anymore to get me started. This is getting out of control. Today, coming home from the grocery store, I was in a white t-shirt and blue jeans, the weather was sunny and warm, a reassuringly ordinary September Saturday afternoon in Northern California. I was enjoying the pursuit of the familiar, my routine, when without warning my body reacted to the remembered sound of your voice, as though you were in the car with me, whispering, saying if we ever made love you would need me to suck your breasts hard and long because you had breast-fed and you needed extra care, extra attention, wanted, needed my mouth on you. And my own nipples suddenly contracted, hard, visible under my t-shirt; you could have taken them in your teeth through the thin cloth; my cunt began to throb against my jeans, the walls of my vagina swelled into a screaming ache, desperate, begging for your hand.

My skin had electrified itself with the very idea of you. I had to pull off the road just to get my breath back.

Okay, I seem to be having a problem with delayed reaction time. But things are getting clearer. Is that why you didn't insist on giving me the phone number? If we ever make love. The last time we spoke, when you asked me if I would come up next weekend and I said, no, we should wait until the airfares went down, I was practical and calm, you remember that? Well, this is why I wanted to talk with you. I believe I have been in error. Like with the phone number. I'm confused, but I'm not that confused.

Why do I think you've been waiting for this conversation? I can just see you smiling, hear your laughter. If I were to ask you, I know what you would say, the same things you have said for the last month: that you love me, that I make you happy. But what does that mean exactly, what does that mean for us, here and now? I have spent the better part of the last ten years learning how to recognize the difference between fantasy and reality. I'm not so far gone that I've forgotten everything. So I'm not getting this. What is the goal and how will we know when we get there?

I'm forty years old. I've been around the block a few times. It's not like I don't know what's happening to me. I do. I just don't know what to do about it. I don't know how to say exactly, but everything seems different, even the way I want you.

You said something about romancing me with sweetness. Tell me what that means. Do I need romancing? Isn't it enough to know I'm in deep trouble already? Isn't it enough to know I walked into my ex's house, started making normal conversation with her, and within ten minutes, *she* was laughing, asking who was this woman in Seattle anyway, and was I aware I lived two states away? Now she wants to know your name.

Isn't it enough I can't get any work done during an intense work period? You know very well when a person is self-employed you just can't take off when you want, you've got to work when the work comes in and be glad for it. I'm not glad and I'm not working. I can't think of anything but you. Isn't that enough? I could ask you to stop, I guess. I know you would.

Well, I could. Like I could tell you I wanted your weekend number. Like I could tell you how my body aches to sleep with you, not to make love, but just to sleep with you, see you at midnight, your hair wild, spread red on the pillow. Well, maybe sleeping wasn't all what I had in mind. I'm a divorcée, remember. My thoughts are not virginal, and neither is my body. I know exactly what I want, I know how to tell you, I know you will listen and go slowly at the beginning but will not hesitate, will make me wait only as a diversion, will touch me lightly only as an inducement to other things, I can feel your hands on me even now.

That's not the problem. Airfares are not the problem. Scheduling is not the problem. The problem is next Monday. What will we do then? Tell me why we are even contemplating this. I have kissed you exactly once. We live two states apart. I'm not moving; I have a business, a mortgage, and a family here. You're not moving; you have a shared-custody child and a career there. So what the hell is going on? What are we doing?

If we were younger, well, if we were younger we wouldn't have these commitments. But it's more than that. We also wouldn't have memories we couldn't get rid of; we wouldn't know how badly we could get hurt. Not knowing how bad it could get, we might not care. We might be making a lot of stupid mistakes very quickly.

Maybe I should speak for myself. I thought about that a lot this weekend. I realize you know this already. I see how patient and how loving you've been. It's been registering. I heard you ask me what I needed to feel safe; I heard you say that we could do whatever I needed, that it was important to you I not feel terrified. I heard all that.

Why does falling in love at forty feel so different? I can't get my mind around this. I'm not having a problem with my body. It's the rest of me. I keep trying to imagine the parts before sex, before taking my clothes off in front of you, and I keep thinking I'd just sit on the end of the bed and weep; do you understand, it hurts too much, the last time, it's too soon, I would just, well, I would just sit there trembling. I know what this costs. I know where this goes, and so do you. It's easier to talk about sex than safety.

Do you want to know the truth? I'm glad you're in Seattle. I just ... I don't know what I'm doing. I'm afraid, okay? And I'm old enough to know it, and grown enough to say so. If this were only about sex I wouldn't be this frightened, that much became very clear this weekend. If we were only about sex, this would be easy.

If I thought there was another way, if I could figure out a way, I would. I can't figure out how to make this safe. I don't know what's in between dating and marriage, between the drowning desire I feel in this moment and what will happen in the future. I don't want to leave my life here. You can't leave yours. I guess this is what it means to be middle-aged: we both have lives we are no longer young enough to jettison. And I don't want to just come up there and sleep with you and leave. I can't. I don't know what to do. What else can we do?

I can't date like I did twenty years ago and I don't want to get married. To tell you the truth, I haven't wanted to fall in love again. The last time I fell in love with someone out of state it nearly killed me, it was so romantic. Talk about phone sex. I was so hot when I got there, she and I didn't even get out of the parking lot. Ever make love for two hours in a small foreign car in a public airport parking lot? I must have been out of my mind. When she dumped me a week later, I did go out of my mind. I don't ever want to repeat that. I don't want to believe in fairy tales anymore.

I look at your picture; I think to myself: it's too late. I already love being with you, even if it's only on the telephone. I try to reassure myself, try to make myself safe. It won't be the same with you; you're not the same woman. For one thing you've already carved your name on a few trees; you don't need my heart. For another, every time I slip into romance you come back, in your very sweet, gentle way, asking questions, keeping me awake, keeping enchantment at bay, offering me a conscious choice. Is that why I feel so naked when we talk?

Is that why it's so terrifying to me? It's not like I've never fallen in love before. On the other hand, I suppose there is a difference between falling and choosing. Now, *this* is scary. My God, this is making me feel like I can't breathe. No wonder I'm terrified to think about what it would be like to be really naked with you if this is what we're talking about.

You asked me to come next weekend. You asked me to choose. Choosing you, choosing me, choosing not being overwhelmed, choosing not to say I couldn't resist, or was overcome by desire, the magic of the moment, the love of my life. They all sound a lot like "Boy, was I drunk last night," when I think about it. I've done that more than enough, wouldn't you say? But walking in boldly on my own two steady feet, and saying yes, I want this, I want you, I want you in my mouth, in my hands, I want you in every part of me, I don't know where it's going but it matters to me just to show up for this, for myself and my own naked lesbian desires, look at me, honest as I can be, whole as I am, broken as I am.

Now that's another story, isn't it?

I just can't imagine, well, sex, sure, that's easy. Sex is mostly the same, isn't it? I mean body parts are body parts. Hands brush. Lips touch. Muscles and skin tighten against that touch. Breath quickens. One of us moans into the other's mouth and we take turns holding on, breathless until we slip over the edge and suddenly time moves in mysterious ways. But it's pretty much standard, isn't it? I'm trying to imagine how it could be different.

What if I just got down to it, like I've had to do this weekend, and admitted how much I've already come to love you? That I don't know what that means yet, and will not know until I hold you in my arms, feel you in my hands, watch both of us, turn fantasy into long moments of reality. Remind me to breathe. You talked about safety. Remind me I am not alone in this, that there are two of us here. Maybe we could talk first; isn't that what grown women do? Talk things over?

What if I were able to make the choice to see where that talk might lead, if I found the courage, not only to try again, but to try anew, as though I had never made love with my eyes open before? What if I walked in with my eyes open and my heart open one more time, knowing you were strong enough to break it open? What if I walked in and told you the truth about how much I want you? What if I was not ashamed of my desire, my flagrant, wild lesbian desire, and I walked in with all of me open? Is it possible I get to do some of my life over, knowing what I know now?

What if I got on that plane next weekend? Would you pick me up at the airport? Would it be after a long day at work and would both of us be tired? Would you take me home and draw me a bath with lots of water, even against the drought? Would you fix me a little something to eat and watch me eat it without saying a word? Would we need to talk, or would we be unable to stop talking, once we didn't have to pay for every word?

Tell me what happens. Tell me how you see it. Your house, what sheets will you have put on the bed? Will there be another place for me should either of us get frightened? Will it be warm enough? Can you make me warm enough? Will you strip me for the bath or will you keep me awake, make me take my own clothes off and stand in front of you, strip myself, bathe myself, you watching, and then, only then, when I am there, right in the moment, will you insist I offer myself to you as a fully conscious choice, full of wanting and love waiting, will you take me then? Will we be able to wait that long?

Will I pull you into the tub with me; will you hold back? How long will you hold back? How long will we talk? Will it matter? When we finally kiss again, will you make the first move, slowly, like you mean it? Will you mean it? When we get there, I'll know.

Will we be too exhausted to make love? Will it matter if we sleep or not? Will you cover me with your body, leave my hands free, so I can push you off if I need to, if I'm not sure I can go right into it? Can we keep the light on so I can see you, it's been too long not seeing you, I want to see every part of you and not just with my eyes, but with my hands and my tongue and my lips.

Light a candle. Show me. Watch me, watching you. If I keep repeating I love you, know it's true. Let me lower myself down on you slowly, so slowly I feel each part of you, pressing my breasts to yours, my lips to yours, brushing slowly against your skin, kissing more slowly than snow melting in the spring.

If I put your hands up over your head and stroke you with the tips of my fingers, will that take too long, will you mind if I trace your backbone with the tip of my tongue, the wet nipple of my breast? How long can you wait before I take your breasts in my mouth? How long can you rock underneath me until you can't wait any longer? How long can I wait to find out?

If I catch your hair in my hands and pull you down on me, will you resist? If I want you to listen to my heart, if I put your ear between my breasts, will you listen to how it beats broken-ly now, how desperately it calls out to you, how terrified it is of your touch, how much power I give you to hurt me just by telling you exactly what is happening inside me, how naked I am, how naked I've been since the moment I met you, how I ache so much for your touch I am terrified to allow even the thought, how I walk around even now, wet as spring, how I can't figure out how I'm going to live without you once you have taken me, once you have pulled my hips into yours, rolled me in your arms, once you have claimed me?

How will you claim me: full hard and soft? All of me, all of whom we both can be, will be, might have been, still could be? If I weep afterward, will you hold me? Will you not get up right away? Do you have any idea how hard it has been for me to never once say, don't go? If you come out of me too quickly and I whisper don't go, will you hold it against me?

If you want to know the truth, I feel delirious just writing this, do you know that? How much have you thought about this? What could we possibly do in the morning? The dishes? I will have to go home sometime. Does that mean I shouldn't come at all? What can come of this, tell me; I want so much, God help me, I want you in my mouth, your hands stroking my inner thighs, I want you to whisper in my ear, your cheek wet next to mine, hold me as close as a dancer, feel the muscles in my ass tighten against your hand, take me hard, take me quick, take me now.

Don't back down. Don't make me these promises with your attention and your own sharp consciousness, don't think this is just about me. Don't think I can't take you just as well. Yes, I want you. I want your face in my hands, my tongue in your mouth, to lick your lips and bite just a little, pull just a little, bring you into my world too, bring all of you into my mouth. Listen, don't think I won't. If I get this far, you'll be coming with me.

I would start with your palms, if you want to know. I'd start there, brushing my lips against that part of you that holds on, stretching your arms up over your head so that all your muscles down to your toes are taut, taut as a wire that will vibrate under my tongue. I will suck you hard, and long, and until your breathing changes and you arch your back, pushing your cunt into mine. I can wait just as long as you can, I can go on longer, I can go anywhere you want me to take you, and I can hold you when you come back, when you weep. But you already know that; this is where we started, weeping.

What more there can be I don't know, but I do know this: I love you, I love being with you, I love how I feel when I am with you. That much is not fantasy. The reality after that is harder, and we both know it, but that much is real, that much has already happened whether I ever kiss you again or not. How easy it would be if that were all we needed to know. The rest takes time, and patience and willingness. How badly we've both been hurt learning this, separating this, growing into this.

The rest? I don't know. Maybe there is some version of dating that can fit us at midlife, between states. Is long-distance dating possible? I don't know.

You want to know what I'd really like right this second? I'd like for us to have made love, and to be tucked into each other, my right leg over your still-wet cunt, protecting, and my left shoulder nestling under your right arm, my head on your shoulder, and my right hand touching whatever I want on your naked, sweaty body. I want you exhausted, and happy beyond laughter, your head back, hair soaked underneath when I comb it with my fingers. I want you to seek out my fingers like an animal, stretching into me and settling down at the same time. Keep your eyes closed and drift off with me.

Forget the dishes. Forget the distance between us. Forget tomorrow morning. Just float with me into the night. Let's get some sleep. Maybe we don't have to figure out our whole lives right now. Maybe we just have to show up and tell the truth. Maybe questions are more important than answers. Maybe the next step will come clear once we've taken this one. Maybe we'll know when we get there.

So what *are* our goals here? I'm not sure what mine is, besides what it always was: to learn how to love one another in a way that's kinder and more honest than the last time we tried, to attempt one more time a conscious articulation of our hearts. I don't know what else there is in life — or what else matters.

One thing I do know: this time will be different because we are different. Maybe there is something to be said for midlife. Maybe we can actually learn from our pain. And maybe you're right about staying in the moment. You once said if we waited to know if any relationship had a future, we'd die cold, hard women, and you didn't intend to. Neither do I.

I'll be there; the plane arrives at 6:30 p.m. I'll wait at the gate. Meet me.

Carol's garden

◆◆◆◆

Chris Strickling

The weathered fencing had turned that soothing shade of gray that happens when wood has withstood the rain and the sun and the wind for several seasons. It matched the gray trim on her light blue house. The patterned brick walkway curved slowly, almost imperceptibly, up to the broad porch, where two old-fashioned metal lawn chairs waited, welcoming. To the side, the overgrown flower garden was moving, alive with bumblebees and a soft breeze. The leaves of the live oaks that shaded the grass from the morning sun were whispering secrets among themselves. It was still early; the summer sun had not yet heated the day.

I pulled into the loose gravel driveway, stopped the car, turned off the ignition, and took a deep breath. I had invited myself out here for a bike ride, and I wasn't sure how I would be received. Hers was the warm body that went with the personal ad I'd answered. She had advertised, "Your mother would approve," and hinted at her love of gardening and books. On paper, she was perfect. When we met that first day at a café near my house, I had walked up the stairs to the waiting area on the porch with a wrinkled written description of her clutched in my palm, wondering what she really looked like.

Sitting across from her at the table, I couldn't decipher who she might be. She was quiet — not that she didn't talk — but her body was quiet. Her eyes were so clear you could almost see through them, the green so tentative it was only a suggestion. Her hair lacked real color; it was the almost-blonde of wheat or sand, and it hung lightly around her face in a disarming way, suggesting a boyish innocence. The jeans, the crisp cotton shirt, and the inevitable Reeboks gave little information about her. She looked scrubbed and healthy. Her voice was low and tinged with a certain sadness when she was off her guard. The lines on her face when she smiled were deep, rippling across her jawline like waves.

We did the usual twenty-five-words-or-less disclosure, using a lot more than twenty-five words, trying not to show our awkwardness. We talked about our gardens, about baking bread, exercise, literature, therapy, politics, parents. We exchanged abbreviated coming-out stories. I watched her handle the clear glass tumbler that rested on the smooth surface of the oak tabletop, watched her squeeze the lemon wedge and drink down all the coolness, consume that tart wetness, and I took comfort in the age that showed in her hands. Tiny wrinkles and brown spots and newly trimmed nails. A woman my own age, at last.

The two hours we spent together on that first day passed so quickly I was surprised when she stood and gathered her things to leave. Driving home in the afternoon heat, I couldn't stop thinking about her hands. They had done a lot of work, there was a roughness to them, but she moved them easily, with a subtle gracefulness.

I waited the appropriate number of days, then invited her out for Saturday night. Exactly on time, she emerged from the gray cab of her import truck, carrying a loaf of homemade bread. A small grin crossed my face, but I kept it to myself. She moved slowly, but her smile was wide. Her black jeans hugged her hips closely, her small waist tucked into them for safekeeping. She wore what was undoubtedly her dress-up shirt, washed yellow with huge indigo flowers, almost Hawaiian. We did whatever people do on a date when they don't know each other; we asked and answered questions until we'd had enough. I got a sinking feeling that I had bored her. I wanted to see her again, but I couldn't find anything to say.

"I'll be talking to you," she said. "I enjoyed the evening."

I wanted to touch her hand, or stroke her face, make some sturdier connection. Instead, I got out of her car, fumbling hopelessly for my house keys.

Meeting women was turning out to be much harder than I had anticipated. The last eight months had been interminably long for me, as I tried to recover from being left behind by someone I loved intensely. My lover had brought up issues I'd never faced, given me about ten days to talk them over, and before I knew it the moving van was pulling up in my driveway, the two husky hulks she'd rented to help at the door. I watched the furniture leave the house, saw the blender and the vacuum cleaner go and I never knew exactly why. Suddenly single again, at forty — it seemed almost too much to bear.

A week passed with no word from Carol. I was confused and irritated, disappointed. Had I talked too much, or not enough? Maybe it was my clothes. Did she hate my femme earrings? Was it the lousy restaurant? I remembered the dating rules I learned in high school. Not that I dated in high school, but I knew the rules. First you ask them out, then they ask you out. It has to go in turns.

I could hear Paul Simon complaining about all the useless things he learned in high school, and when I picked up the phone it was slippery in my sweaty, unsteady hand. The first three digits were easy, and even the next two, but those last two sixes just wouldn't come. Over and over again I repeated the litany of those numbers, then finally dialed the whole thing, praying for an answering machine. My little speech was all written down and could be delivered in less than ninety seconds, so I was ready. Then I heard, "Hello," at the other end of the line. Where did my voice go? I only had that minute and a half prepared, and nothing I'd rehearsed started out with "Hello."

We got through that inane conversation somehow. I suggested a bike ride. In July, in the Texas heat, that means early morning. This morning, exactly on time, I arrived at her house in the country, emerging from my compact import car, nervous, carrying the Florence King book I'd promised to share. It has to go in turns.

The front door opened before my feet hit the ground, and she padded down the walkway, barefoot, smiling a slightly restrained smile, shoes in hand. The navy shorts hit her legs just above the knees, and her pale pink polo hung close to her chest as she moved.

"We'll have to get started pretty soon if we're going to ride before it's hot," she said. She opened the gate to retrieve her bike while I unhitched mine from the car rack and fumbled with the water bottle.

Minutes later we were riding along a riverbank beneath ancient cypress trees on a narrow road whose bends moved us gently through the lush green morning. Purple spider wart bloomed near our feet, bayou moss hung overhead. The water was high for this time of year, but the road was clear. Talking was easy where the road was flat; the hills forced a breathy silence. Riding single file on the shoulder of a small stretch of highway, I watched her from behind, the muscles in her calves bulging from the effort. As she shifted her weight on the narrow seat, the perfect curve was obvious. I could feel my heart rate change. It was too hot. I stopped the bike and grabbed for the water bottle, then peeled off the t-shirt that had covered a tight black tank top. Sweat was streaming shamelessly down my chest, circling the slopes of my breasts. I caught her eyes on me, registered the interest, and we rode on.

Back at her house, red-faced and out of breath, we rested.

"Come over here, I'll show you my garden," she said as she lifted the latch to the gate of the high wooden fence.

I stepped out of the heat into the shade of a cottonwood, and stopped short. This was no ordinary garden. The whole enclosure was a private explosion of color and smell. Dozens of raised beds with wooden sides offered a smorgasbord of herbs and flowers. Giant lamb's-quarters were verging on bloom, the anxious lavender buds waiting. Pink verbena and yellow cosmos spilled over the wooden slats, interrupting the path of a blooming Carolina jasmine. Standing cypress, which she had stolen and transplanted from the creek bed under cover of night, trumpeted their orange blossoms, stealing the glory of the burgundy celosia that grew nearby. Mounds of rosemary encroached on the space allowed for comfrey and Mexican oregano. Tomato plants shared their stakes with vining honeysuckle. The remains of a small glass hothouse made a miniature meditative temple near the garden wall. The heat vibrated the air around its smooth glass panels and quick darts of light splayed off its still-shiny metal joists.

I sat down beside it, enjoying the olfactory banquet. The phone rang, and as she turned to go I watched her legs move up the steps of the deck, noting the glide of her arm as she opened the door. She returned carrying two tall glasses of water, slices of lemon and lime perched on their rims. At her invitation, I rose and followed her to begin the official visitor's tour. She knew these herbs and flowers as friends. She had stories of all their origins; this one a transplant from her mother's garden, this one a migrant from a neighbor's yard. As she talked, she reached down without thinking to extricate a weed that had strayed into an herb bed, and my hand found its way to her waist. When she stood, she leaned the weight of her body into mine, but turned her face away. I gently pulled her in closer and brushed the damp hair from the back of her neck with my other hand. She turned her face to mine and our cool lips met, exchanging the taste of lemon and salt.

"Let's go inside. Its hot out here," she said, as she pulled awkwardly from my embrace. The rest of the tour could wait.

Once through the French doors, she rested on an old brown Lazyboy that sat by a window in the broad, open room that faced her garden. She was settling in for something, but I wasn't sure what. I sat on the narrow sofa opposite her, wondering what it was that she wanted, watching her body for clues, calmed by the soft whir of the ceiling fan. She began to talk about herself. There was a slow unfolding of her past, a condensed version of her last relationship. I learned the source of the sadness that sounded in her voice. I asked her a lot of questions, which she answered with determined candor, then asked me many of the same questions. It had to go in turns.

Is this what we were supposed to be doing? I couldn't tell if she really wanted to let me know her or if she was just uncomfortable doing anything else. She seemed so at ease there, safe in her big chair.

"Carol, I'm getting hungry," I said, recognizing my own restlessness. "Is there somewhere we could go for lunch?"

"There's a place down on the creek. It has an outdoor area. The food isn't great, but it's cheap and the view is worth the trip."

We decided to leave the bikes behind and walk down to the café, which was nestled amid a stand of cypress trees that hugged the creek's curve. As promised, it had a wide, covered porch with clean white tables. As we passed through the door and entered, I pressed my fingertips gently into the damp groove of the small of her back like a gentleman, guiding. She noticed the touch and turned to check the expression on my face. I smiled my courtly smile. Once we were seated on the open porch, conversation again came easily. The food was fine, the service unremarkable. I made my foot run into hers underneath the tiny two-top, and her eyes told me she enjoyed the flirtation. When the check came and we both laid money on the narrow black tray, I felt her hand touch mine just for a moment, too long to have been unintentional.

"So, can we finish the tour of your garden now? I'd love to see the rest of it." I didn't want to be sent home.

By the time we reached her house again, she was complaining about her back.

"Are you all right?"

She coughed out a little sighing laugh. "I get this cramp in my back sometimes. Nothing serious, just enough to bother me."

"I know a good cure for cramps," I said with a smile.

"I bet you do," she replied, as she opened the gate for us. "Let's sit over here under the tree for a while and catch our breath."

We sat down on the grass under the cottonwood tree, glad for the shade. I rested in a wide, flat space between two of her flowerbeds, she was stretched out on her back at the foot of the beds, trying to get comfortable.

"Can I get you one of those pillows from the couch?" I offered, and she nodded yes. I grabbed a throw pillow and the old bedspread that covered the couch.

"Here. Stand up for a minute and I'll put this underneath you."

On her back, with the little pillow wedged under her neck, an arm folded across her face to shield her from the brightness of the sun, she was finally comfortable.

"All you need now," I teased, "is one of those broad-brimmed straw hats with a lavender bandana wrapped around it. You'd be the perfect lesbian gardener."

"I have the hat, but no bandana. It's over by those tools," she responded, gesturing toward the shed.

"I bet you do," I said, smiling.

Again, we talked. I watched her chest rise and fall as she spoke, saw how the cloth clung to her breasts, and I felt disconnected from our words. After a few minutes, I lost the focus of the conversation. I couldn't resist the urge to lie down beside her, to stretch my body next to hers and slide my hand up under her shirt to rest on her low, flat belly.

She laid her hand on top of mine, pressing lightly to get my attention. Too much, too soon, so I took her hand in mine. The smell of rosemary filled my head as I ran her fingers across my lips. Her breathing slowed as she relaxed. We stopped, laughed a little nervously, and waited. When her eyes told me she was comfortable, I moved my hand down across her thigh and carefully stroked upward along her side. My skin was tingling — it had been a long time since I'd touched someone. I rested my hand on her chest, in that wide flat place between her breasts, and felt the rhythm of her breathing. I could feel her trembling.

I pulled her over on top of me and discovered her wet mouth, tasting less like lime and more like woman than before. Her body was slender, her muscles still defined, but she was soft to the touch. She framed my face with her hands, and, guiding my head back gently to expose my neck, she nuzzled it with kisses. Touching my chin with her tongue as she moved up, she found my mouth again and stayed there. My hungry hands traced the contours of her back, caressing that perfect curve, and the kisses went deeper. She was ready. There was a scramble to remove our clothes, the predictable awkwardness, then our full-length longing side-by-side, and the taste of her nipples as I urged them erect. I moved my hand down her legs, letting my palm rest between her thighs. She moaned and spread her legs wider to allow me in. Her supple skin yielded easily to probing fingers. I was careful at first, unsure, but the arch of her back told me she wanted more. We started a dance, her body meeting each surge of my hand, the rhythm shifting to some unknown, inaudible beat.

Our eyes met; there was urgency in her gaze. I moved over on top of her, my thigh between her legs, pressing. My tongue made circles on her breasts, each tug on her nipple making her harder. I felt my body respond with a rush of wetness. My mouth got dry. I slid down the length of her body, my legs open, across the rise of her pelvis, across the sharp bend of one of her knees, and we both sighed. Her scent drew me in, and as my mouth found her, wet, silky, and smooth, I raised my eyes to glimpse the landscape of her hips, the low rolling valley of her abdomen, the rise of the round hills of her breasts, the arch of her neck. She was mine.

When the intensity of her orgasm washed over her, there were small tears, shed shyly, and a heavy sigh. In the silence that followed, her grip on my arm became painful. As I stroked her hand, she gradually let go, turning to reach for me. I was stirring, moving, primed by her arousal and her release. As she touched me, the breeze blew the scent of summer's last honeysuckle across our bodies, hardly competing with the ripe smell of our sex. Her energy shifted, her body pushing into mine with intense need. Rough hands moved purposefully, teeth and tongue pressing flesh. Inside and outside, she surrounded me with a frenzy of desire. Stunned by her hunger and encouraged by her passion, my body exploded quickly into a convulsion of pleasure, and we wrapped ourselves together in a mingling of exhaustion and contentment. It had to go in turns.

It wasn't long before the insects and the heat prompted us to move. I retrieved the sweating water glasses and we revived ourselves.

"You were delicious," I said, as I plumped the pillow that had been under her head and handed it back to her.

She took it from me with a slow hand, sighing, "Thanks," and handed me my clothes.

Suddenly conscious of the fact that we were both naked in her backyard, we went inside and dressed. Somewhere between the shorts and Reeboks were more kisses, embraces, tongues and whispers and small, contained laughs. I glanced at her wall clock and knew it was time to go, knew I didn't want to go, didn't know what to do next.

Driving home, I couldn't stop thinking about her hands, couldn't let go of the taste or the smell of her. The smells of the garden faded, but I carried the scent of her on my hands. When I opened the door to my house, I could see the blinking red light of the answering machine.

There were three calls. The first two were hang-ups.

"Hi. It's Carol. Listen, I do want to see you again." Her voice wasn't completely steady. She was nervous. "I'll be in town on Tuesday. Can we get together then?"

I couldn't help but smile as I picked up the phone to respond. She was inviting herself over. It had to go in turns.

Siesta

✦✦✦✦   *Cynthia Perry*

Pat kept telling me to take a vacation because I work too hard, I don't know how to relax, I'm too stressed out. When she gave me a ticket to a Mexican resort for my birthday, I knew that her sudden concern for my mental health was probably tied to her new interest in the woman next door. She always likes to get me out of the way when she's on the prowl. That's okay. I'd just as soon be somewhere else at those times. But why in the hell did she have to pick this goddamned Mexican island, where the biggest event of the day is the setting of the sun?

Not to mention it's hot as hell and the rays burn me to a crisp if I stay in the water for more than a couple of minutes. And there's absolutely nothing, *nothing* to do except drink, sleep, or sit at this little café on the beach, staring out at the sea. Pat thinks this will relax me, but she's wrong. It's going to drive me crazy, and I'll probably kill her when I get home.

Anyway, this is more or less what's going on in my head when I notice a Latin family sitting across from me at a table with a big umbrella. The man looks straight out of "Miami Vice," real slick, with an expensive suit and an arrogant expression on his face. He's reading a newspaper in a way that makes it obvious that it's just an excuse to ignore his wife and kids. The little boy and girl look like they're both under five. They're very quiet and solemn, probably because a formidable-looking maid is hovering over them, whispering all kinds of evil threats. But what really gets my attention is the mother. She seems as restless and bored as I am, I sense that, like me, she's ended up in this place against her will. She keeps staring out at the horizon as if she expects to see something there yet knows, at the same time, that it will never appear.

Her lips are full and moist, slightly parted, and under the flimsy silk of her shirt I can see her breasts rise and fall as she breathes. Her skin is the color of cinnamon. I don't have to be near her to know that this is the way she smells, too. The heat has brought a slight sheen to her bare arms and legs. I know that her skin is moist to the touch, and hot. Her hair is dark, long, and riotously curly. She has partially tied it up in the back, but it has escaped and cascades around her face and neck. I watch the breeze lift her curls and gently set them back down, tenderly, like a lover's hand. Her mouth is wide, her cheeks sharply etched, her nostrils slightly flared. She isn't exactly beautiful, but is both sleek and powerful, like a wildcat. She has legs that go on forever; full, womanly hips; a narrow waist; and large, heavy breasts.

I realize that I'm staring at her cleavage, lust written all over my face. I'm trying to get myself under control and force myself to remember that she's somebody's wife and mother, for God's sake — probably one of those ultraconservative, ultrareligious Latina housewife types — when she suddenly turns to me and smiles. Her eyes are laughing, knowing, amused. She knows what I've been thinking; I see it written on her face, and I feel naked, caught in the act. She gazes at me serenely, with nothing more than mild interest. I feel myself turn red. I choke down the rest of my margarita and stumble off to my cabaña, where I throw myself down into my hammock and vow to stay there for the rest of the week.

Let me say something here about these hammocks. In this part of the world, hammocks are as important as food and water. In the heat of the afternoon, nothing feels as good as dozing in one of these big, soft cocoons, suspended in midair, gently swaying in the breeze. Mine is on a shady patio surrounded by all kinds of flowering tropical shrubs that smell divine. Combined with the sound of the ocean waves, the heat, and the booze, you can float along for hours on end, waiting for night to come.

Anyway, here I am in my hammock, and I can't stop thinking about this woman I've seen. I close my eyes and see her lips. I imagine what it would be like to kiss her, to touch her. I feel a familiar tightness and burning between my legs, an aching pressure building up. I think some more about the woman's hair falling down in little tendrils around her neck. I think what it would be like to kiss that neck, to taste the salt of her flesh, and to hear her soft moans. I run my hands across the tips of my breasts, thinking of how it would feel to touch hers. My nipples get hard and my clothes are suddenly too tight, too restrictive. I pull off my t-shirt and bra, and slip out of my shorts and panties. My hands travel across my stomach and down between my legs. My eyes close. I slide my finger back and forth across my clit and then slip it inside my cunt, then out again — slowly at first, then faster, harder, until I feel like I'm on fire. I think about what it would be like if it were her hand on me, in me, caressing me; what her leg would feel like if it were to slide between my legs; what her mouth would feel like on my nipples; how her tongue would feel if it were to trace a path across my stomach and down to my cunt. And

34 ✦

all the while, I imagine how *she* would feel, how *she* would smell. The fragrance of the flowering shrubs around the patio is spicy, the way she would be. Their exotic scent wafts over me, reminding me of the way skin smells after a day in the sun and wind and salt water. I bite my lower lip and wish it were her mouth on mine. My cunt is so wet, so hot, I know I could come any minute, but I want to wait, to enjoy it as long as I can. I lessen the pressure of my hand, sigh, and gently stroke the lips of my vagina, the tender flesh between my thighs, spreading the heat of my cunt along my legs, across my stomach, back up to my breasts.

Suddenly, I feel an ice-cold drop of water on my chest, and then another, tiny splashes of coolness, one quickly following the other. My eyes fly open and I see her standing there, next to my hammock, a drink in one hand and a dripping ice cube in the other. She smiles, sucking the ice cube she had been dangling over me, then drops it back into her drink, as if it were the most natural thing in the world to do. She takes a sip, then offers the glass to me.

"Why don't you have some," she suggests in a husky voice with just the slightest trace of an accent. "You look hot."

She laughs a deep throaty laugh and then hands me the glass. I stare at her, flabbergasted. I think I must be dreaming. She just stands there, her pelvis pushing against the fabric of the hammock, her hand playing with the ropes, rocking me slowly, her upper body bent slightly over mine. She watches me, smiling a slow, patient smile. Then, she fishes out another ice cube from the drink, holds it to her mouth, and sucks it for a while before bringing it down so that it almost touches my breast. She holds it very carefully, so that when I breathe, the ice barely grazes my nipple. I gasp and she withdraws it, but then she smiles and begins to trace a tiny circle around my nipple. Carefully, with the same precision, she moves it to the other breast and does the same thing, thoughtfully, as if it were important to her that it be done just so. The ice burns against my skin but, at the same time, feels deliciously cool. Currents of electricity run down to my cunt and back to my breasts again. She kneels at my side, her right hand still caressing my breast with the melting ice cube as her left hand moves to my head. She stokes my hair with soft, rhythmic motions and looks deeply into my eyes. I feel like she might pounce on me and eat me for dinner. I wish she would. After a minute she smiles, puts the piece of melted ice back into her drink, and takes a sip.

"It's better now," she says. "It tastes more like you."

She leans over me, kissing me very softly on the corner of my mouth. Her lips are cool and wet from the drink. They smell like lemon candy. She lifts her mouth and moves it to the center of mine, where she presses gently but firmly against my lips. I feel her take my bottom lip between her teeth so lightly that it feels like a kiss in a dream. My lips open and her tongue slides into my mouth. It touches my tongue lightly, then withdraws again, playing across my lips in a leisurely caress. She lifts her head for a second to look at me, then smiles as if to reassure me. By this time, I don't care what her story is, whose wife or mother she is, or what in the world she's doing with me, as long as she's going to be with me for a while. I reach up and pull her head down to mine again, and this time we kiss fully, deeply, until we're both breathless.

She unbuttons her blouse and takes it off, then slips out of her cotton skirt. She climbs into the hammock with me, wearing nothing but an expensive black lace bra and black silk bikini panties that look fantastic against her dusky skin. The hammock folds around us and we lie on our sides, touching each other's face and looking into each other's eyes. We kiss again, and again, as our hands reach out to explore each other's body. I run my tongue lightly down the side of her neck, around her ear. I kiss the tender spot behind her ear, which makes her gasp and then giggle. I slide down and kiss her nipples through the sheer black lace of her bra. The stiffness of the material against her breast excites her. I like the feel of it against my tongue, and the hardness of her nipple pushing against it. I suck the nipple harder, and she moans. I take it gently between my teeth and pull, lightly at first, then a little harder. Then, I free the breast from its hold and take the tip of it into my mouth as my other hand slips beneath the lace of her panties.

She responds immediately to my touch. She bathes my fingers with her milky wetness, so that they slide across her and into her with ease. I work first one, then two, and then three fingers inside her. I feel her expand around them, grasp them, pull them in, thrust them out, and pull them in again, in a slow, measured rhythm. My hand plays across the lips of her vagina, my fingers tease her clit; they slide back inside, then out again. Her back arches, she presses against me, her face buried in my neck, her breath ragged in my ear. I reach down with my other hand to rub her clit while I plunge my fingers in and out of her, and she puts her mouth to mine, imitating the movement of my fingers inside her with her tongue. She makes little moaning noises deep in her throat that drive me crazy. I know she wants me as much as I want her. I don't need to know anything more about her. There isn't a nook or cranny, a line or fold, a patch of skin anywhere that I don't know, that I haven't touched or kissed. I don't know anymore if I'm touching her or touching myself, or whose hand is doing what to whom. It doesn't matter. We're beyond caring.

"I want you to kiss me down there," she whispers. "I've always wanted that. I want to know how it feels. I want to have your mouth on me. I want to be inside your mouth."

I immediately go down on her, but I like the idea of stretching it out a little and making her want it more, so I take some time and do it right. For me, the best part is wanting it, waiting for it to happen, when you're absolutely sure of what's coming and you know it's going to be great. So I leave those sexy black silk panties on her for a while, and I begin by simply rubbing my cheeks against them, feeling her pubic hair bristle beneath, smelling the cinnamon-and-clove scent of her cunt, luxuriating in the softness of the lace and the woman. I run my nose down to the spot where her clit is and nuzzle her softly. My lips are poised over her cunt. I touch her through the black lace. I wet the lace with my tongue and find the lips of her vagina, the slit of her cunt. I press my tongue inside. The silk of her panties is so sheer that when it gets wet it's barely there. But it *is* there, rubbing against my tongue like another tongue, soft but a little rough, too, just enough to feel really good. I move my tongue up and down her slit, pushing it inside as far as the silk will let me. Then I move my tongue to her clit, which is standing up erect and rigid in anticipation.

The lace is drenched with her wetness and with the wetness from my mouth. I take it inside my mouth and suck it, like I'm dying of thirst, and then I push it aside, feeling my mouth on her naked flesh for the first time. She tastes salty and warm, like the tropical sea, but has a flavor that's all her own: spicy and a little bitter, like café con leche with a dash of cinnamon. She arches against me, pushing herself against my tongue, moving her hips in rhythm with my mouth, a series of little thrusts that never miss a beat, that never slow, never stop. She takes my head in her hands, holding it gently, her fingers wrapped around my hair. She guides my tongue firmly to the place she wants it to be and holds me there, moving against me faster and faster, her breath coming in ragged, hoarse pants. She's biting her lips to keep from screaming, but she can't hold back little cries of pleasure as she comes. I keep my mouth still then, but continue to press against her until I feel the throbbing subside. I take one final taste of her and pull myself up to look into her eyes.

They are glowing like hot coals. Her hair half covers her face, which is bathed in sweat, and her lips are red and raw. But she looks happy, very happy. I move on top of her and spread her legs. I press my cunt against hers and begin to rub against her, up and down, up and down, sliding across her smoothly and effortlessly, feeling the wetness of her cunt and her swollen clit against mine. Our bodies are dripping with sweat. Our breasts touch, the nipples of one body rubbing against the nipples of the other, our stomachs slick, our hips joined, our legs entwined. She reaches for my lips and kisses me deeply. She takes my tongue inside her mouth and sucks on it, pulling me inside her. She opens her legs wider to accommodate me, then wraps them more tightly around my hips. I continue to rub and press into her, caught up in my own pleasure. She arches her back and pushes her pelvis forward, thrusting it toward me. Then she puts her hands on my ass and pulls me closer to her, holding me firmly against her, forcing our cunts against one another, at just the right angle, so they melt together as one. I feel her growing wetter, or maybe it's me. I can't tell where she ends and I begin. We're the same body, we feel the same desire, the same pleasure. I move, she moves with me. She cups my breasts in her hands and squeezes them hard, a long slow squeeze that goes straight to my cunt. She pinches my nipples between her fingers, a slow, deliberate movement that sets me on fire. She bites my neck; she traces her tongue up to my ear and licks the spot behind it. She plays with my earlobe, taking it between her teeth, biting it softly.

"Come here," she says. "I want to taste you. I want to feel you against my mouth." She slips down beneath me, between my legs, pushing me up and positioning me over her face. She pulls me down to her, taking me into her mouth. She does everything I had done to her, and more. She goes on for a long time, and if she really *was* new to this kind of thing, all I can say is that she seemed to have a natural talent for it. When we're finished, we lie facing each other in the hammock, bathed in sweat and other bodily fluids, exhausted but content, and suddenly tired. Once again, I'm aware of the sound of the sea, the heat, and the breeze through the palm trees. We drift off to sleep, locked in each other's arms.

When I wake up, the sun's going down. The sky's red, and I'm alone in the hammock. I think I can still feel the heat from another body next to mine, but there's no way to be sure. My body is tender and slightly bruised, but I can't tell if the hands that touched me were my own or someone else's. I smell cinnamon and cloves but, of course, that could just be my imagination. I'm groggy and a little confused. Then I see the empty glass bearing a dark red lipstick mark on the ground next to the hammock. I never wear red lipstick, but I know someone who does. A smile crosses my lips, and I vividly recall that afternoon's siesta.

"I don't think I'm going to mind this vacation at all," I say to myself. "Pat's right. I do need a vacation. Vacations can do wonders for a person."

The immortality of dreams

✦✦✦✦ *Katherine Fugate*

It was raining — one of those rare occurrences in Southern California that causes complete memory lapse in the motorist's ability to drive. The driver of the Hyundai in front of me kept hitting the brakes like a whore in church reciting the Hail Mary. The car made a right-hand turn into the D.G.A. building. Figures. The neon orange vests with the neon orange sabers gestured me into the outdoor parking lot, nicely avoiding the indoor multileveled structure on the left.

"Why can't I go inside instead?"

"We have to fill this one up first."

"Why?"

"Please park."

"You may not have noticed, but it is raining and I would like to park indoors." Shapeless cars were honking behind me, their lights glaring disapproval. Ever so polite, I responded by not moving at all. Finally, the saber swung left, allowing me the grace of the covered sanctuary. Sometimes it works.

It was opening night at the Gay and Lesbian Film Festival. Men had more earrings than women. Women had less hair than men. I was meeting a friend. I scoured the backs of heads for her slight frame and sleek black bob. I finally spotted her looking at the artwork hung in the lobby. She is an artist.

Jonae and I hugged our hellos and started for the theater. And then by some divine doorbell, I heard *Her* coming from across the room. She wasn't supposed to be here. Her platinum blonde hair swung over one eye, she strode forward in her black cowboy boots, brandishing a roguish grin. One step behind her was her lover, a thin rail of a woman as bland as tapioca. Determined, *She* headed toward us, tossing her mane with distracted nonchalance. She was beautiful. An equine species emerging from the sea. And (as usual) she robbed my heart of its beat.

"You almost ran into me back there, Katherine," she pronounced. I was startled. She drives a Hyundai, *that* Hyundai.

"Well, Diana, your driver's license should read 'cannot drive when raining' instead of 'cannot drive without prescription glasses.'" She was silent for a moment. Then she burst out laughing, a red hue coloring her pale cheeks. She hugged me and I felt the weight of her heavy breasts commingling with mine. Will it always be this way, I wondered? This beating of the chest. This soft inhalation when she touches me. This epicurean repast.

My love for Diana was my own. Sweet and pure and oddly sexless. I worshipped her like those who did her ancient Greek namesake. To imagine the taste of her lips, the pressure of her touch was too much. A sacrilegious conceit. Instead, my love for her grew holy. I kept memories of her laugh, her hands, her movements, her essence trapped in a bottle. It languished there, fermenting into a bittersweet perfume.

Tickets in hand, we joined the theater line. Diana stood directly in front of me and I studied her back, the curve of her hips. Full and sensual. A painter would want to paint them. A sculptor to sculpt them. A lover to love them. In me, I felt something changing. The first emergence of a seedling breaking through the hard-packed earth. I reached my hand out and rested it on her hip. My fingers, vines spreading across the curve of her bone. She looked at me, seeking a question from my unexpected touch. "The line is moving," I gestured. A quizzical eyebrow lifted. A misplaced nose sniffing out any abnormality. Her lover called her name and she ran to join her. I wondered, Was she satisfied?

We sat dead center. Diana's lover, Diana, me, and Jonae. Two older lesbians sat next to us. Encased in gold and carrying keychains branded "Mercedes," they were on the hunt. They looked each of us up and down and then quickly dismissed us. They hit the next row. I laughed out loud, amused by such obvious predatory behavior. Jonae, who also caught the act, joined in.

A woman with big hair suddenly stood up and addressed the crowd. "The following presentation is the first half of a four-hour miniseries previously aired on the BBC. The film is based on the life of poet and novelist Vita Sackville-West, who was married to Harold Nicolson, and her affair with another woman, Violet Trefusis. That this movie dealt with lesbian issues both intelligently and explicitly and aired at 8:00 p.m. in England is remarkable." She went on to ask for money as most speakers tend to do. "Membership to the festival entitles you to..."

Lights out.

Vita and Violet are childhood friends. They chase and court one another in genuine bliss. Vita wears the pants. As they grow, they acquiesce to conventional society, Vita (now wearing a dress) marries and moves away. The years pass and they gain experience and wisdom. Vita becomes a poet. Violet more bold. Lying in front of a fireplace, Violet finally speaks of her love for Vita. Words absolved, she leans back on the sofa in relief. Vita paces the room like an expectant father. The words spoken become living tissue, attaching themselves to Vita with a tremendous pull. She soon is kneeling beside Violet, holding her hand. Violet leans toward her, eyes fastened on her lips. A mere inch away from Vita's mouth, she speaks. "I have waited so long for this moment. I can't believe it is actually here." They kiss, slowly. Tenderly. Soon they are on the floor, the fire crackling in the background.

The movie continued but I did not. Too many ethereal drugs. My senses were overloaded, my body reeling, my seat too confining. I looked at Diana in the dark, sitting so regally. I became Violet, she Vita. But their passion was too sweet. Too good. Too directed.

I leaned back in my chair, eyes closed. I stretched my legs out straight and taut. My jacket laid across my body, lengthwise. Blurred, the images came slowly into view. The room is barren, white, no doors and no windows. One could say stifling. The whiteness of death, of immortality. Diana is standing by a bed, hovering slightly. The bed is very old. An aged paramour, with a wrought-iron headboard. The mattress is worn and simple. The bed has one rumpled white sheet, the cotton soft from many washings. Slowly she takes off her white t-shirt and drops it to the floor. I watch until she is wearing nothing. She stands defiantly before me, daring me to touch her, knowing I will not. I disrobe almost clumsily. I face her.

I pulled out of this fantasy almost as soon as it began.

Vita and Violet's love has progressed. Now they lie by a pond and a tree. Idyllic lovers from an art photograph. Adoringly they look into each other's eyes. But Vita's husband has returned and she loves him, does not want to hurt him with this image. They run across meadows and gardens until they reach Vita's house. Muted, Violet watches their exchange. When she can stand it no longer she tells them she is going to take a bath.

I thought of Diana's lover now. The folly in fantasy. The danger in letting it progress. I read somewhere that the reason there is so little morality in dreams is because no one gets hurt. I wanted Diana in this dream, and decided I would have her. I had wanted so long it no longer hurt. The tired muscles of my heart no longer an abnormality, but an echo. Always there, yet faintly. Gingerly, I reopened the door. I shut my eyes again in that charged theater and let myself go. On this plane, I would have her.

I am lying on her, moving slowly. She wants to kiss me but I won't lower my head. Instead I keep moving, my hipbone rotating between her legs. I can feel her getting wet, her hair swelling with moisture, saturating my skin. Slightly, I increase my speed. Her breath quickens almost imperceptibly. Her hands wrap around my waist, pushing me against her harder. I shift so I am no longer touching her directly. She tries to pull me back, but I refuse. Instead I thrust my hands into her hair, turning her face toward mine, and I kiss her hard. My tongue searches inside her mouth, probing each corner, sliding past her teeth. Her mouth widens to take me in and I suck her tongue, pulling it into my mouth. In and out. In and out. An erotic vacuum. Her hair covers my face and I cannot breathe. I kiss her, the asphyxiation exciting me. Beads of sweat form along her hairline. Almost faint, I pull away.

In the theater, Jonae noticed my fixed stare on the screen. She jerked me awake. My muffled response puzzled her. I crossed my legs and felt the wetness there. Uncomfortable, yet comforting. My clitoris was undulating, rhythmic contractions. I tightened my legs and ass. With one sweep of my hand I touched myself. My clitoris sprung to life, eager and wanting.

I dropped my hand under my jacket and left it there, gripping my inner thigh, my legs now slightly spread apart.

I tell her I want to taste her. I want to be inside her. I want her. She says nothing, but instead tosses her mane back and forth. I want to bring out the animal in her. To do so, I must cage her. Trap her. I reach down to the floor and grab her t-shirt. Easily, I rip it in half. Before she can argue, I tie one hand to the bed frame. I avoid her face and reach across for the other. Do I dare blindfold her? No, I decide I want to see her pale blue eyes widen. I want to see her when she comes.

I stand at the end of the bed and start with her feet. Even though they are free, they remain rigid and straight, as if tied. I kiss the feet that I have never seen outside of her black cowboy boots. I move upward, slowly touching the skin. I'm amazed by its warmth and tension. I almost let the moment drop. Do love and lust intertwine, or do they turn their backs upon one another? When I was a child my mother told me that the angels (after all their shooting of golden arrows) turn their heads away when people make love. A joke without a punch line.

This slow, languorous lovemaking becomes tiresome for me. Takes too much time. I reach for the insides of her thighs and kiss the flesh there. Musk oil and patchouli. Jasmine-tainted incense. My favorite place to get drunk. She moves forward, offering herself to me. I lick her but never where she wants. What she needs. My hands reach over my head and clasp her sides, kneading the flesh, grazing across, up and down. I raise myself up, basting my skin with her juices, until I reach her breasts. I lower myself onto each one of them, brushing my juices on them, basting her with me. I rotate on her breasts until I feel them harden inside me. I move downward until the hardened nipple is on my clit. I rub myself there until I feel myself beginning to come and I stop. I decide we will come together. I suck her breast, tasting my juices. I circle her nipple with my tongue. I suck harder. She cries out. I bury my head between her breasts, rubbing my clitoris against hers. Hard, I fuck her. Up and down, grinding. On the edge of orgasm, I halt, leaving us there, on the precipice of nowhere.

A black screen. My reverie broken by a broken film. The lights came on in the theater. Jonae looked at me. "Are you sick? Feverish?"

Diana stretched, turned her body closer to mine, and looked at the projector behind us. "Just a reel change he screwed up," she informed us. Her hands impatient, drumming. Within seconds, the theater was dark again.

Violet is alone in an empty house. Vita stalks her but hides from her. She is dressed like a man. Violet enjoys the game and continues the hunt. But the house is big, empty save for odd pieces of furniture draped with drop cloths. Heavy curtains blowing in the wind. She grows tired and nervous. She calls Vita, but there is no answer. Violet goes from room to room, floor to floor. It is getting darker. She enters a room and Vita is waiting in the shadows behind the door. Violet calls her name. Vita grabs her from behind. Violet screams. A hand covers her mouth. Another pulls her petticoats down. The hand thrusts inside her quick, without mercy. Violet struggles. Vita pushes her down on mounds of rough blankets and lowers herself on top of her. Violet succumbs.

I reach for the lights and turn them on. Diana wants them off but I want to (I need to) see her. I look at her body fully for the first time. The pale nipples, the dark curly hair contrasting with her feathery white skin. Beautiful. Waiting to be harvested by me. I am all hands. Touching her everywhere. Grasping her. Biting her. Sucking her skin. Savoring the salt of her sweat. Diana arches her back. She lifts her head and tries to see me. Looking down, she sees my head devouring her, my fingers inside her. I look up and meet her eyes, my head barely lifting from her. She smiles and throws her head back. I keep drinking.

I turn my fingers inside her in a circular motion, and feel her wrapping herself around them. Alive, her world pulsates. A living organism. Here I find the sea. Wet and moving. Turbulent and thrashing. Her tide crashes onto my hands and I want to swim inside her. To drown if I must. I withdraw my fingers and put them in my mouth, sucking. I enter her again and withdraw, this time putting my fingers into her mouth. She sucks them eagerly. Her hands want to touch me and she thrashes.

"Untie me now, I want to fuck you too."

I untie her. She rolls on top of me. She puts her hands behind my head and kisses me. I can taste her. She sits up and kneels over me. She grinds her body on top of mine. It doesn't take much. She moves, our clitorises touching, locked into each other. I reach out and pull her body toward mine, dragging her upward, until she is sitting on top of me. My tongue reaches out and she writhes. That cloying feeling again. My nose buried in her pubic hair, my tongue toys with her clit. It is throbbing, red and enlarged. I suck on it slowly, then harder and harder. She stretches upward and then over me. Her arms grasping the headboard. She rocks forward and backward. My tongue waiting for each thrust. She shudders and shudders. I feel her vibrating. Her body a succession of tremors. She tries to move away but I hold her and rock her there. Making her come. And she does. And I do. She says my name. *She says my name.*

Lights on.

I realized my breathing had stopped. I looked down and saw my hand between my legs. I felt the pressure I had placed there. I was not breathing. I realized that I was about to come. Palpitating with fear, palpitating with desire. Diana was reaching under her seat for her jacket. Jonae was putting hers on. With a deft, knowing motion, I moved my hand in quick circular movements. My legs tensed, straight and proud. Diana's eyes rested on my taut legs. She knew what I was doing without looking higher. This tableau was frozen: Diana staring at my legs, me staring forward, save for the rocking motion of arm and hand. In a few short breaths, it was over. In Diana's eyes I saw her questions, her curiosity, and her disapproval. Around me, I did not care who else had seen. For in this room of blinding light, I had come.

for my Muses, Melissa and Denise

Gardenias

♦♦♦♦   *Willyce Kim*

When I was growing up, my father would warn me to stay off Hotel Street. Just in case you've never been to Hawaii, Hotel Street begins a couple of blocks from the Honolulu harbor, winds its way along a canal, which is occasionally used by small fishing vessels, curves abruptly back toward the pier through condemned housing projects, and disappears into the open-air fish market. My father wasn't talking fish when he raised his voice about Hotel Street. He was talking "red light," sailors, and the great Wah Ta Ta.

"The great Wah Ta Ta?" laughed Nan as she patted my thigh.

"The great Wah Ta Ta," I soberly replied.

"The haoles made up the story, and all Hawaii fell for it, even you."

"Of course I fell for it! Who *wouldn't* fall for the legend of an exotic widow from China who could suck up beer bottles into her vagina — paff, paff — just like that. She actually headlined around here, you know," I said, pointing to a group of boarded-up buildings. "You want to take a look around?"

"How much time do we have?"

"As much time as you want."

"Don't play with me, Johnnie!"

"My flight doesn't leave for hours. We'll do this now, then a little of that, and maybe more of that."

"As long as we're not rushed," said Nan glumly. "I hate backseat quickies."

"I know that, baby. I know," I said soothingly.

"Yeah, yeah, you do," replied Nan, sucking her thumbnail. "But before you leave tonight, promise me one thing, Johnnie."

"Name it," I said, pulling into a parking space.

"The hotel elevator."

"You want to do it in the hotel elevator?"

"It makes me hot just thinking about it," Nan said, squinting into a dry-goods store.

I stared at Nan and watched her move up the street in front of me. It's a little hard to understand, I know. That there's only this sex thing between us. But we found each other through the personals. We met for the first time in a café in Austin. She had tea and I had a double cappuccino. We didn't talk much. I remember touching Nan's hand (her real name is Nancy), following her to the bathroom, and getting shoved up against the sink. We did it there, slipping and sliding against the toilet tank. The encounter was memorable, too, for the line that had formed by the time we opened the door.

Nan collects tolls on the Golden Gate Bridge in San Francisco. On the weekends she moonlights as a cocktail waitress at a place called ChiChi's. She likes to tell me about the special babes she's served just as she is getting ready to go down on me.

For our vacation this year, we had decided to tour my home state. Nan wanted to do it on each of the seven islands. These past two weeks had been filled with great sights and greater sex, but I couldn't afford to take any more vacation days, so I was flying out ahead of her.

Last year we did Texas, her home state. As a tribute to her idol, Nolan Ryan, we had sex in the Astrodome on the pitcher's mound, even though Ryan was now pitching for the other Texas team, the Rangers. It was Nan's idea, not mine. She pulled it off by convincing her Uncle Louie, the head groundskeeper, that I was researching domed stadiums for a West Coast publication. By trade, I'm a research assistant to a cluster of reporters at the *Cal State Gazette*. I flashed my press credentials. They worked better than a bag of gold; to our amazement, Uncle Louie turned over his set of key cards to us. Every time I see the Astros play, I stifle a laugh and think about the two of us grinding away on the Astroturf. I especially remember Nan slowly raising her ass over the pitching rubber, waiting for me to fuck her. Sometimes when it's slow at work I get tossed a bone. I wrote a nice piece about my visit to the Dome. It was featured in the Sunday leisure section. I guess you might say Texas proved inspirational.

Nan took my hand as we crossed a small intersection. There wasn't much foot traffic; no sidewalk vendors or tourists — only occasional locals passing us on their way to the fish market. After walking several blocks, peering into Chinese herb shops and boarded-up dance halls, I could feel myself beginning to flag under the tropical sun.

"How about a drink?" I suggested, running my fingers through my hair. "A drink would probably make me smile in all the right places."

Nan peered over her dark glasses at me. "You're wilting, Johnnie," she said. "On your own turf and you're wilting!" She brought my hand up to her mouth and rubbed it slowly against her lips. Someone honked his horn. Nan shrugged her shoulders, then very slowly brushed her leg between mine. My breathing began to quicken. Somewhere in the distance I heard another horn. We were standing under a sign that read "Blue Light Hotel." The building looked as if it had been condemned years ago. I stepped away from Nan, into the shadow of the hotel, and took off my dark glasses. "Whoa!" I said. "The last time I checked, queers were still listed at the bottom of the Honolulu popularity poll. People disappear down here all the time and no one cares."

Nan pursed her lips and stared off into the distance. "Let's get out of the sun," she said, pointing to a bar named Lena's. "You know, last night seems so long ago, I can't remember how it feels to be in a dark room with you." I shook my head and dropped Nan's hand. A slight breeze blew against us, raising Nan's nipples invitingly against her shirt. Biting my lip, I stepped back into the light. I slipped my dark glasses on, deliberately grazing Nan's nipples with my arm. "Buy me a drink," I said, as we drifted lazily down the street.

"I'll buy you a river so I can drown in you," Nan replied as she pushed up against the old, weathered door marked "Lena's Lounge."

Immediately, as we stepped inside, the intoxicating smell of gardenias and cigarette smoke engulfed us. A tattered Union Jack hung from a large beam directly above the entrance. Standing under it while our eyes adjusted to the muted light, I noticed an old jukebox. We crossed the deep, rectangular room, past a small stage, to a long mahogany bar. I pulled out two stools and wiped the perspiration from my brow. Two small windows were ajar at the very back of the bar. Overhead, a fan generated more noise than breeze. A pair of dice and a cup sat next to a stack of ashtrays. At the opposite end of the bar, an elderly woman in a long muumuu played solitaire. "What'll it be, girls?" she said, flipping cards deftly along the wood.

"A bottle of carbonated water and two glasses," said Nan, strolling over to the jukebox.

"Only water we have is tonic, okay?"

Nan looked at me and nodded. "Lots of ice," she called, climbing onto the stool next to mine.

"Want some quarters?" I asked, fishing into my pockets.

"Well," said Nan, tapping the counter lightly. "It's interesting. The only music they have is Big Band and swing. You know, the stuff from the Glenn Miller–Benny Goodman era. I wonder if this was a dance hall," she mused as our bartender pushed forward two tall glasses filled with crushed ice, and a large bottle of chilled tonic water.

"You girls lost?" the bartender asked as she obligingly poured our drinks. "We neva get too many customers unless they lost," she continued in the island's pidgin English. "This one tough area to be lost in."

I took a large sip of my drink and rubbed Nan's ankle with my foot. "Lena?" I asked. "Are you Lena?"

The old woman plopped several maraschino cherries into our drinks. The fragrance of gardenias floated up from her heavily scented wrists. "Lena dead for many many years," she said, shaking her head. "The Machado family, her folks, ask me to look after things. So I come every day."

"What's your name?" Nan asked, swirling her finger in her drink.

"Everybody call me Eva. My real name too hard to say. No exact meaning from Chinese to English!"

"I'm Johnnie and this is Nan," I said. "Johnnie's a nickname. My parents called me Jennifer." Eva smiled and lit a cigarette. I don't think I ever saw her draw on it. It just sat in an ashtray next to her and burned like a stick of incense.

"Well, Eva," I said, suddenly feeling much cooler, "here's to you." I raised my glass and clinked Nan's. Eva nodded and watched us drink.

"Why don't you bring us another bottle," Nan said, finishing her tonic. "We're buying for the house."

"We're buying for the house and the great Wah Ta Ta," I added, taking a look around the empty room.

"Yeah, the great Wah Ta Ta," Nan echoed, placing her hand upon my thigh.

Eva reached below the counter and set another chilled bottle before us. She wiped the bar down and refilled our glasses with ice. "What you know about Wah Ta Ta?" she asked, lighting another cigarette.

"Only what everybody else says," I replied.

Eva placed a shot glass on the bar. She filled it with whiskey and slowly began to sip it. "Wah Ta Ta dance here," she said emphatically, tapping the bar. "Many times she dance here."

Nan and I exchanged quick glances. "You saw her?" I asked, leaning forward into the counter. "You actually saw the great Wah Ta Ta?"

Eva nodded and raised her glass to her lips.

"Was she beautiful?" asked Nan, squeezing my thigh.

"So beautiful," Eva replied, "everything stop when she walk into room. Men pay big money to see her show. This room, no can breathe. Too much smoke, too much men, when Wah Ta Ta come to dance."

"Eva, tell us," I slowly asked, "is it true? Was she as big as everyone says she was? Or was that just bullshit?"

Eva poured herself another shot and placed it next to the burning cigarette. "Come," she said, patting both of our hands. "Come." Nan looked over at me and shrugged her shoulders. We slid off our stools and followed Eva into a small back room.

A tiny table holding several framed pictures was crammed up against a bed in the corner. Above that, a glass cabinet jutted out from the wall.

Eva carefully opened both doors of the cabinet. "Look," she said. "See for yourself."

Nan and I peered in. We saw beer bottles and candles and ben-wa balls the size of a fist. There were leather dildos, rubber appendages, and carved ivory penises as thick as my forearm. There was also a curious item — a long glass tube balanced delicately within a metal stand. "What's this?" I asked, touching the glass with my hand.

"Emperor's teacup," Eva replied.

"Emperor's teacup," I slowly said, staring at it, pulling Nan to my side.

"Once, this all belonged to Wah Ta Ta. She bring out maybe one, two, three things a show, and use sometimes alone, sometimes together."

"Together!" Nan murmured under her breath.

"Emperor's teacup the best," Eva continued.

"Men pay big money to see Wah Ta Ta come onstage, but no one ever touch her. They pay more big money for drink in teacup."

"Shiiiit, Nan," I said, rolling my eyes. "Wah Ta Ta could ejaculate!"

Eva smiled at both of us. "She catch in cup and sell to highest bidder. Once some big shot pay in gold coins."

"She was good," Nan said, shaking her head.

"She was da best. Da best."

I licked my lips and suddenly felt very thirsty. "How about bringing us some drinks, Eva," I said, pressing a twenty-dollar bill into her hand. "A couple of tonics, and a shot of rye for you. Why, we'll stand right here and have our toast."

"Okay, Johnnie," she said. "You two sit on bed and wait."

Nan and I watched Eva close the door to the room. I was keenly aware of Nan's leg rubbing up against mine. "Why don't we?" she whispered, touching herself. "You know you want this."

"What about Eva?" I asked as Nan climbed onto my lap.

"What about her?" Nan replied, pushing me back onto the bed. "She's not coming back for a while, Johnnie. Don't you know, she would have never left us alone in this room..."

I stared at the glass cabinet. Nan hovered above me, biting her lip. "Okay," I said. "Okay. What will it be?"

"The balls," Nan firmly replied, pulling down two silver spheres.

"The balls," I whispered into Nan's ear, my tongue running down the side of her neck to her breasts. "Take off your clothes," I ordered, as Nan's hand slid between my legs.

"Only if you're wet," she replied, lifting off my shirt.

"You're the one using the balls,"' I said, rolling over on top of her. "Come on, baby, let's see what's going on down there," I whispered, spreading Nan's legs and unzipping her shorts.

"Goddamn it, hurry," she begged as I pulled down her pants and unbuttoned her shirt.

"Give me the balls," I gasped, fumbling with my Levi's.

"Here," she said urgently. "Here!" I raised up on one elbow to fit the cool metal between our thighs and felt Nan cup her hands around my ass. "That's it," she said. "That's it!" as we rotated feverishly around the balls. I slid a finger into Nan. Then another. Nan threw her legs apart and moaned. I brushed the balls against her wetness and pushed them deep inside her. Back and forth, we rocked together, the bed creaking loudly against the wall. I don't know how long we were there or when day turned into night, but as we were coming, I knew from the hint of gardenias in the air that Eva was watching us.

Cinema scope

✦✦✦✦   *Alice McCracken*

I'm an assistant manager in a movie theater. The hours are lousy and the pay is even worse, but it's a great job for a dyke — navy blue suit, man's shirt and tie, black socks and shoes. And since I've been a sucker for movies all my life (yes, I go all the way back to Esther Williams and Doris Day), I still can't believe that I get to watch them all for free.

The only real drawback for me is the nonfraternization rule. A lot of nice college-age kids work behind the snack bar; they hang out together and have a good time. At the end of the shift, they head for the nearest bar, while I stay to close up the place and then go home alone.

Most of them are straight, anyway, so I'm probably not missing much. I've spent most of my life trying to fit in but not fitting in, and I finally know who I really am. One of these days I'll find someone for me.

Meanwhile, I get tempted now and then. After all, I'm human. This summer, my boss hired a cute gal. Tall, long legs, flowing hair, chocolate brown eyes, and a smile that would light up a whole movie screen. And self-confidence like you wouldn't believe. Janelle. The first time I saw her, when she reported for training, crisp and clean in her new apron and visor, I really got it bad. I throbbed between my legs. I would invent things to say just so I could have a word with her. I made sure to bring change for the cash register; I answered every question. She would smile and call me "Ms. Richardson."

All very proper. And I had no business even noticing her. I'm a rookie on the management team; all I need is trouble with the staff. The boss knows I'm a dyke, and it's okay with her, but if I cross the line with an employee, man, I'll be out of here in a minute.

So, to get back to my story, it's the end of the summer. We've been busy with the big blockbusters, and I've been hustling on my shifts to keep up with the paperwork, make the change, answer the phones, help out where needed, and keep things running smoothly. On this particular night I'm helping clean the theaters — we've been a little shorthanded on my shift — and I'm trying not to notice in the half-light of the auditorium that Janelle is sweeping up next to me.

"Hey, I found a quarter," she laughs with glee. She is a college student and needs to count her pennies.

"Lucky you," I quip. I avoid looking in her direction as she stoops to pick up the change off the floor; I know her strong, athletic shape by heart. If I don't look, maybe I won't cream my pants again.

So, I swallow back my desire and pound my way through the evening — first upstairs to police the women's restroom, then downstairs to get the phone, then back upstairs for some supplies. Soon I'm wringing wet in my wool and polyester. On nights like this I'm never sure if it's passion, menopause, or just plain heat.

One time, on my umpteenth trip back down the stairs, I think I see Janelle looking right at me from the cash register, a big smile on her face. My heart skips. She winks. I stop dead in my tracks. Then she says, "Rodney, don't forget the cups — we're almost out." I haven't even seen Rodney, just behind me, on his way to the stockroom.

I sigh and grab a sweep set. The lobby needs attention. I flick a few popcorn kernels into the bucket, grumbling to myself. I try not to notice Janelle talking and laughing in the background. I ask myself what I'm doing here, a middle-aged woman in a job designed for kids? And I answer that I came here to find myself, and I am doing that, however slow and painful it sometimes seems. So shut up, my friend, and quit complaining.

Finally, the shift ends and I start my closing procedures. The doorman is mopping up behind the snack bar, the computer is printing out a summary of the day's receipts, and I am headed to the projection booth to shut it down.

I get excited just walking into the booth. Movies are like a religion with me, and the booth is truly sacred. It's big and dark, with a heavy fire door that normally stays locked. I feel privileged to have a key, and I tend to tiptoe when I enter. We have a projectionist, but because of the long hours we are open, the managers are the ones who have to close down for the night after the last film ends.

We're a fourplex, and two of the movies have ended already. I leave the fire door ajar to let in some light from the hallway. Flashlight in hand, I go to the first projector, open it up, loosen some screws to remove a part, open several sprockets, close her up, and then stabilize the film on the platters. I repeat the same process with the second projector. I move quickly, but I'm always very careful.

Now that I have two projectors secured for the night, I sneak a peak through the glass at the screen where one film is finishing up. It is a steamy R-rated love story that opened last weekend. I haven't had time to watch the whole thing yet, but when I close I always hit just the moment of the climactic sex scene. So I stand there, enthralled, while the hero does his thing with the heroine. Being me, I'm watching the woman. I'm standing there feeling the sweat under my collar, looking at her breasts, her thighs, the curve of her stomach, following as the cinematographer focuses in. The hero doesn't exist for me, only the body of the woman, and in my mind I am there with her — touching her, making love to her. And as her nipples harden, as she sighs and groans, I am sighing and groaning, too. Call me a voyeur if you want, but a lonely old dyke has to get her kicks wherever she can.

While I'm standing there, engrossed in the passion on the screen, I am startled by a voice beside me. Very quietly, "I've always wanted to see the inside of the booth." It's Janelle.

I look at her, my eyes widening. I swallow. "You shouldn't be in here," I whisper. My voice is hoarse with distress.

She puts a hand on my arm. "Don't worry. Everyone's gone." She is so self-possessed, even here in the booth. She steps closer to the window, taking in the scene on the screen below us. "Ooh, that's steamy, isn't it?"

I feel myself coloring. "Yes," I laugh awkwardly. "It's kind of hard to ignore." Despite my apprehension, I am pulled, mesmerized, toward the screen again. I watch the bodies sweating, gasping, moving against each other.

At the same time, I am very conscious of Janelle, who steps very close, until she is just inches from my side. "She's beautiful, isn't she?" she says of the starlet on the screen. "Nice breasts, a mouthful." Then she laughs, that free, open laugh she has. "I bet you have nice breasts hidden under that awful jacket." She reaches abruptly for the button on my blazer.

Surprised, my heart beating rapidly, I back away. "Janelle!"

She laughs again. "Relax, I've clocked out; no one knows I'm in here. I pulled the fire door closed — you have the only key, right?"

Things are moving too fast. "But—" I see my job doing a fast fade.

"No fraternization, right? Well, this is my last night. School starts Monday, and I have another job for the fall. So relax, nobody will know." She runs her fingers gently along the line of my tense jaw. My heart is pounding with passion and fear; I am throbbing between my legs.

I struggle with thoughts, words. "Janelle, you can't—" My voice sounds like gravel.

"I can't what?" She is shoving my jacket off my shoulders. It falls to the floor. I am frozen to the spot. "You think I don't know what you want? You think I haven't seen your eyes watching me with that hungry look?" She kisses me gently on the cheek, then on the forehead. She is tender. "You've been so careful all summer, but your eyes give you away. I could feel you caressing me, could see you following the line of my body when I moved."

Behind us the lovers are fading out and the credits are rolling. Here in the booth, her visor has hit the floor, along with her apron, joining my jacket, everything barely visible in the dim light cast by projector bulbs.

Where is my management training now? I am not thinking at all. I am a mass of sensations, succumbing to her seduction. Down below, the janitor has begun cleaning theater one, two lies empty and shut down, the credits are rolling in three, and four has ten minutes yet to run. Here I am standing in the dark with this tall, tanned young woman, who's taking me, possessing me. I have no will, no power to refuse.

Off comes my tie; my shirt is being unbuttoned. I feel dizzy. Her hand goes to my breast; the nipple has come to burning attention. I stand there, torn between passion and terror, weaving.

I feel her sparkling brown eyes on me, laughing at my distress. She takes my hand and places it on her breast; I feel its firm roundness and my hand is at once on fire.

Suddenly I grab her and pull her close to me. "Janelle, I want you, I can't deny that, but we can't be doing this." As I listen to myself speak, I feel I am acting out some melodramatic scene from the screen — yet this is really happening, to me, right now.

She laughs. "We can't? Forget the rules, Ms. Richardson. You're a dyke, remember? You're out of bounds by definition. Let it go, relax, let this be my farewell gift to you. Let me make love to you."

We are on our knees, and I don't care that the carpeting is old and smelly from years of service in perpetual darkness. I feel only her muscular body pushing against mine. The popcorn and candy, the patrons, the computer, the janitor, the booth, the credits — none of it exists.

Janelle pulls me down, and I am on my back on the projection-room floor. My clothes are in piles around me. Her mouth is on mine, her tongue reaching, pushing its way between my teeth. My body shudders. I feel her reaching all the way into my heart, my soul. Everything is melting away. All I can do is groan. "Oh, Janelle."

Her mouth caresses my breasts and I shiver. As she sucks gently and then tongues each nipple, her hand moves down my body toward my pubic hair. She parts my lips with her fingers and discovers the warm, moist region within. Gently she slips her finger inside the opening to my vagina, and a sensation like a hot burning rod runs through me.

My mind struggles to hang onto a sense of reality. "Janelle, Janelle, who are you?" I gasp.

She puts a finger to my lips. "Just a free spirit," she says, "wanting to give pleasure."

She strokes my cheek. "I have watched you trying so hard to get it right, trying to be there for everybody. You take this all so seriously; I wanted to see you smile, just once."

"Oh, my God, Janelle," I gasp in ecstasy, as she moves her long, slender fingers slowly in and out my vagina.

"Tomorrow you'll come in to work with a smile. That tension will be gone from your face, and everyone will know you got something tonight. And you'll never forget me — I'll always be here with you in the projection booth, every night, when you shut it down. It will be our secret, and no one will ever know it was me."

Now her mouth is on my clitoris; she finds the head, and I groan with pleasure as she teases it with her tongue.

The final projector clicks as the tail end of the film slides through; it shuts down, and I know the curtain is falling on screen four. The patrons will be leaving.

"Janelle, I must—," I struggle to begin.

"No, Ms. Richardson," she laughs, "not yet. The climax always comes before the credits, you know that."

She strokes my breast with one hand; the other slides in and out my vagina, and her tongue tantalizes my clit as sweat pours off my body. My muscles burst their tense hold in one glorious come.

◆◆◆◆

Uncounted moments have passed. I am holding Janelle gently in my arms, listening to her relaxed breathing. I don't want to let her go. I dread the moment when she will slip into her clothes, pass down the stairs and out the door — and out of my life.

Somewhere down below the janitor is finishing up his sweeping. He will soon be looking for me, wanting paper towels or cleanser from the storeroom. Reality pushes its way back into my consciousness.

As if sensing my changing focus, Janelle begins to stir. My inner voice screams, "No, don't leave!" yet I force my arms to release their grip. I lie still, tolerating the itch of the carpeting beneath me, keeping my eyes closed, as Janelle pulls on her pants and shirt.

Then, feeling cold and vulnerable, I start to move, to speak. Janelle leans down and once again puts a finger over my lips. "Thank you, and good night," she whispers gently, kissing my cheek.

And she is gone.

I climb into my uniform, torn by a multitude of emotions. Thankfully, I have tasks to orient my actions. I set the last two projectors and flick off the electrical switches. Red lights blink off and the motors stop; the booth is silent. Silent, and dark.

As I stand in the doorway, giving a final glance to see that all is in place, I realize that something is different. Janelle was right. The booth now belongs to me in a special way that it never did before. I can replay our personal magic in my head, like a movie, whenever I want or need.

I shut the door. I am going home, alone, but a secret smile tugs at the corners of my mouth, and I am content.

Cunt cult

✦✦✦✦ *Dorianne Erickson Moore*

I am one. One of the cult. The cunt cult. We are underground, a very fitting place. Obviously we're not concerned with fitting in, not in the regular sense, at least.

Going underground has been one of my favorite political actions. Fingers going underground, below the surface, into the deepest path of a woman. It's the most radical reason I have to continue, the most extreme road I've been on.

We join when there is no moon, when the only light comes from within: the phosphorous wetness of a woman, glistening, showing all heads bent the source of our strength, our songs, and our most savage instincts. Many have lost these, but not us. We are the cult. The cunt cult.

Cunt, a word we whisper over and over, in our corporate jobs, the supermarkets, the bars, on the streets. A whistle, a murmur in the air. Hot, moist air of summer sweating from our pores. *Cunt, cunt:* This mantra moves our mouths. Jaw pushing forward, tongue thrusting with the final sound of a *t.* We hope others become surrounded by the sound, the glowing heat, the moist embrace of a cunt. Sometimes we recognize others. Some are spontaneous converts who've picked up on the word and the chanting. They aren't quite sure why they're saying it and can't help the soft pinkness that spreads across their cheeks, necks, and down their chests. These we guide gently.

Others have been part of the order longer. These we recognize by the outward serenity and insight that comes from their chanting and the countless ceremonies of cunture, the most important practice of our cunt culture.

I remember my first cunture ceremony. I was young and looked even younger, but was ready and reaching for my first taste of a woman. I had heard stories, passed down from woman to woman, but these were only mouth-to-mouth resuscitations of an often intentionally well-buried past. Throughout the centuries women like us have been persecuted, their practices declared illegal. But this has always been a part of our herstory, so we are used to surviving during repressive times. Exactly how our foresisters kept alive back then, we're not sure. But they must have, for their strong sense of survival has been passed down to us, from hand to hand, from hand to cunt, from cunt to mouth.

It was the coldest night of the year. November 30th, like a tattoo across my breast, I will always remember. It is my second name, as clear and clean as my legal one, this illegality that lives with me.

At the time, the local network was small, and only one had found me. Gripping my hand, taking a strong interest in its length and narrowness, she pulled me out of the darkness, out of the crowd and onto the dance floor. I didn't know what was happening at the time, but I learned quickly. Her firm push, which steered me backward and in circles under the soft lights, made me deliriously dizzy. She tightly gripped my belt and yanked me closer. Then she pulled me by my cunt and led me swaying outside to her truck. It was just the beginning of my virtually dark and silent instruction. At first the movements and sounds were small and the light was dim. Eventually things would change and I would understand the true essence of what was to happen, of what I was to become, on that late-November night.

◆◆◆◆

Wind sways the curtains and sends in a hit of chilly air, which traces my skin sharply. I rise, calm, and walk across the cool, creaking wood floor. I stretch. Reaching up, I pull my body loose, and the rap on the door comes. Sliding open the lock, I allow her in, this handsome woman on the edge of fifty. She looks up at me, her light blue eyes glinting and her slow smile scattering my thoughts. Though seven inches taller than she, I feel short. Her close-cut blonde hair is lighter than mine and it frames her pale skin with an edge of other-worldliness. She is dressed in Levi's, a warm jacket, a t-shirt, and black cowboy boots. She tosses down her red backpack and then shakes off her jacket. I lock the door. As usual the sixty-year-old door sticks and I have to slam it shut. The sharp crack makes me jump and I look over to see her smiling at my shaking hands. I slide them into my back pockets and wait. No words yet. Do I talk first? Does she?

She says, "What's for dinner?"

Is this a trick question? I go for the easy answer and lead her into the kitchen, where I have set out a simple meal of bread, cheese, and fruit. I've been much too nervous to cook anything. She sits at the table. I sit. She thoughtfully chooses an apple wedge, slowly pushes it into her mouth, and sucks on it, savoring. My shaking hand starts its reach for the food and then jumps when she bites down on the apple with a hard snap. I manage to get down a bit of bread and cheese, knowing more than ever that I'll need lots of energy. I eat quickly and nervously. When I finish I wait for her to complete her torturously slow and suggestive meal. She licks her fingers clean of fruit juice, bites off pieces of bread and cheese with decisive and salacious movements. She chews slowly, thoroughly, and I sit and wait.

Then she leads me to my bedroom. She's never been here before, but knows where it is. She tells me to wait and goes for her backpack. Breathing slowly, in and out, I try to stay calm. After coming down the hall she lights the candle on my nightstand. Again I wait for a signal. She sits on my bed next to me, looks up my length, and says quietly, "Take off your socks."

I lean over, do it, and feel the cool wood floor underneath. She pushes me to a standing position, facing her, and says, "Unbutton your shirt."

I do this also, carefully and smoothly. A sliver of my ghostly pale skin glimmers against my soft black shirt and reflects the low candlelight. Through my large, uncovered bedroom windows I see the early evening sky sprawled out behind her, a dark purple-blue, underlined by a few deep pink clouds. We are very high above the neighboring canyon and only the tall trees can see in. An owl hoots softly, a mournful soothing sound. She reaches up and grabs my belt, pulling me close, her lips level with my belly. She runs a hand slowly and surely up the exposed V of my skin. Raising both hands to my shoulders, she roughly pulls my shirt down over my arms and then tosses it to the floor. My small breasts seem almost silver in the eerie air and I shiver from the power, more than from the cold: the power of her. She moves my hands to my breasts and has me cup them, her hands covering mine.

"Feel this?" she asks, squeezing me squeezing myself. My erect nipples poke through my fingers and brush hers. She notices this and tightens her grip, pinching my nipples, causing me to shake slightly. Leaning forward, she traces down my stomach with her tongue, leaving a glistening trail of wet. Pausing at my Levi's, she releases my hands and rips open my jeans, tugging them down over my hips. They fall to the floor and I step out of them. She slides her tongue down to the tops of my white cotton Jockeys and stops. She grabs my butt, kneading me.

Pulling my underwear tight, she says, "Touch yourself."

I slip my hand down my front and test my swollen cunt. She grips my ass tighter. Reacting, my fingers push aside my outer lips and slide into a slick softness. I close my eyes, absorbed in my cunt. My knees shake. She shakes me.

"Enough. Taste it, now."

She pulls out my unwilling, gleaming hand. I stroke up my belly and chest and cover my face with the salty wetness, licking my fingers: good. Through the soft brush of my eyelashes I see the glow of my moisture, caused, I assume, by the reflection of the candle flame.

"Take these off, too," she commands.

My underwear is the only thing I have on, so I figure she means that. I hook my thumbs under the sides, flip them down off my hips, and step out. She coolly looks at my completely naked body. Just then a sharp breeze comes in from the dark night, causing the candle to blow out. But the shine of my wetness remains. My amazed eyes follow a ribbon of faint light down between my breasts to the dusky glow that is my cunt. My brownish auburn cunt hair curls from the warm moisture seeping out of my pores, and a trickle of light runs down my inner thighs.

"Very nice," she murmurs, running a finger through my lower lips. I catch my breath as my body jumps forward, aching to take her fingers, or perhaps her entire hand, inside me.

"Not yet," she says. "Be patient."

She removes her finger and runs it slowly across her cheek, my shimmering wetness marking her. She takes a deep breath, slowly inhaling my sweet smell, in and out, satisfied. Again I wait for a signal. She pulls my legs apart and raises her boot-clad leg between my thighs. The black leather rubs me, yet she beckons me to be still.

"Take my boot off."

I grip the boot in my hands and slowly pull it off. She motions for me to turn around, indicating that she wants me to bend over, with my back to her. She strokes my ass. In response my body pushes down on the black leather.

"No," she scolds, squeezing my behind.

I squirm, wanting to rub back and forth. But I wait, and she waits, stroking me, calming me, then pushes me off with her boot captured between my legs. I set both boots at the foot of my bed. She stands up next to me and grabs me around the waist. Her hands run the length of my spine and she settles at the back of my neck. She then pulls me close and kisses me for the first time that night. Her tongue pushes apart my lips and trips inside, circling the inky darkness of my mouth. A deep moan rises from my belly and she grips me tighter, pulling me down onto the bed. Her mouth travels down my neck to my breasts. She circles my left nipple with her tongue and grips my other one between her fingers. The contrast of wet and pressure is disorienting and causes my fevered body and mind to drift even farther away. Sensing this, she pulls back and takes a long look at me. The sudden disconnection of our bodies is like a slap of cold water. I snap back into the present.

"Now," she directs, "you may take off my clothes. Start with my shirt."

I sit up and gently pull her t-shirt up over her shoulders and set it on the dresser, folded, of course. I reach and touch her warm, ripe breasts and she holds my hand to her, squeezing her soft skin, moving inward to grip her nipples as she had mine. I witness her first signs of enjoyment as she moans softly with pleasure. She runs my hands down to her jeans and helps me tug them and her underwear off. My gaze lowers to her silver-gold cunt hair, almost luminescent in the darkness, a hint of an even brighter light to come.

I can't help but stroke the soft crinkly hair, and I allow my finger to graze lightly along her inner lips, as my hand feels the warm wetness of another woman for the first time. She grips my hand, running it up and down her cunt, showing me her most sensitive, glinting places. She allows me to watch her pleasure. I dip my fingers in deeper and then pull out some of her wetness. I spread her cunt, her glistening pool of light, rubbing around her clit and labia, darting to the edge of her vagina. I move up her belly and to her breasts, leaving shimmering finger trails in my path. Then, as if she's decided it's enough for now, she rolls me over onto my back. Leaning over me, her length against mine, she moves down my body.

"Now," she says, her hand tripping through my cunt hair, causing my entire body to tense, "let's have a look at you."

Her head bent, she parts my lips and begins her exploration of a place only I had been intimate with before.

"How lovely," she remarks, rubbing her fingers against my protruding, dripping lips.

The room is silent except for my increasingly rapid breathing and moans. She moves in on me closer and deeper, her fingers probing my swollen, glowing insides. Her tongue coaxes my clit along at a quick pace. My hands grip her hair and begin a dance to the rhythm she has set in my lower body, which has taken over my entire being.

I am lost. My world has widened and narrowed to only this ancient melody beating faster and faster. Blood runs to my cunt until I have no conscious control over anything. My body has taken over. She has taken over. And giving in to her, my cunt pounds with her pulsing fingers. My body reacts violently as it comes and she holds me down, receiving my tremors, gripping me tight and then soothing me until I am calm.

She moves back up to my face, trailing my wetness up my body to my lips. "Very nice," she whispers, her lips moving against mine, bringing me a taste of my own sweet saltiness.

Looking at her face and down my body, I notice that the trail she has left gleams brighter, leading to a phosphorescent glow at my cunt.

"A nice light, isn't it?" she says. "As time goes by it will become brighter and brighter." She touches the source again, causing my hips to rise and rock. "Some more?" she asks. "Let me see how you do it."

She lies on her back and instructs me to hover over her, my cunt to her face. Reaching up, she parts my lips, letting a bit of light spill out. Looking back at her, I see the light on her face and I am thrilled by the sight of her intense absorption in my suffused cunt. She strokes me urgently, and I rock back and forth. She inserts two, then three fingers inside me and then grabs my hand, moving it to my clit. I rub my fingers in a familiar stroke and I suddenly know just what she wants to see me do. It doesn't take long for our moving hands to bring me to a second quivering orgasm. After observing my technique, she seems satisfied, and I move off to lie next to her. Clasping my cooling body to her she waits until my breath has steadied.

Nothing said, I read a readiness in her body's pulse. I lean over her and kiss and bite my way down her skin. Lengthy moans escape from her. Pausing at her cunt mound, I tentatively touch this most sacred ground.

"You may go down on me," she allows.

Shaking with excitement, my hands part her outer lips. The soft beam of brightness emanating from her cunt illuminates her pink, pulsing core. I lower my tongue to her and taste another woman for the first time. She pushes down on me, wanting more than my stroking tongue. I insert one, two, then three fingers. Traveling her inner cunt, I test and marvel at this soft but strong beating chamber. She pushes down on me again, wanting more inside her. I reach up and grab her left breast with my free hand and squeeze her nipple. She moans and her cunt opens even more.

"I think I'm ready," she gasps.

This is what I've been waiting for, the signal, the motion to complete the ceremony, although what we are to do, I still am not sure. I wait with exhilarating tension.

"Come up here. It's okay, you can pull out for a moment," she reassures me, catching my confused look as I wonder how I can stay inside her and move up at the same time.

Her cunt relaxes its grip on my fingers and I slide out. I look at my hand, which is coated with the bright sheen of her moisture. As she gazes down at me I'm sure she sees it glowing from my hand, reflecting onto my awed face. I move up to her. She grips my shoulder and looks into my eyes, her piercing blue gaze testing and evaluating.

"Are you sure you're ready for whatever I ask you to do?"

Without hesitation, I answer, "Yes."

"Very well," she says, "get my backpack."

I pull it onto the bed and watch her reach inside. She brings out a tube of thick liquid.

"Spread this on your hand," she directs.

I coat my left hand with the slick lubricant, enjoying the warm slipperiness. She motions me down between her legs and brings my hand to her. Again I slip two, then three fingers into her, yet she seems ready for more. My fourth finger also moves inside, and the further I go in, the more she expands.

She slowly instructs, between strokes, "All of it, put all of your hand inside."

Pausing for a moment, I adjust my hand by folding my thumb inward and squeezing my hand smaller. I remember her inspection of my hand when she first pulled me out of the crowd. I know now she wasn't only checking my fingernails. My hand seems the perfect size to move into her, and with a slow push I find myself up to my wrist in the warmest, most glistening glove I've ever felt. She groans as I completely fill her, and my hand begins a slow twist inside.

Her breath comes in short gasps as her hips rock from side to side. The strength of her pull is overwhelming and I stay anchored to her, to this woman, this teacher. She embraces my hand with what seems to be the very pulsing and pounding heart of her. My other hand touches her swollen and seeking bead of a clit. My light strokes increase in speed and pressure, keeping time with my shaking buried hand. As my hands move in sync through her thick, wet wilderness, they respond to her shaking and swelling, and I become an extension of her cunt, of her heart. Her tremors run down my arms, through my chest and belly, and into my cunt. My cunt grasps for something of her and settles around her leg, squeezing and rubbing. She lets go of a long, haunting howl. Her body shakes faster. Seizing me tighter, she pulls me in hard. Our bodies throb into a shuddering orgasm, which surges from her into me and back again.

When her clenching cunt relaxes, leaving an imprint of her lines and life on my hand, I am allowed to pull out. With my hand comes a flood of iridescent juices. This white light easily illuminates the lower end of my bed. As I look down at her glowing cunt and my gleaming hand, I fall in love with the most beautiful natural light I have ever seen. And I realize, like the deepest-sea creatures who live with little light or oxygen, surviving virtually on their own life source, that we too bring life from almost nothing. This is what me must do. There is nothing else.

"The glow lasts for a day or two," she says. "Be careful where you take it. Take these," she continues, tossing me a set of butter-smooth black gloves.

I raise them to my lips, tasting and smelling a leather finish very different from what I have known, and yet, at the same time, newly familiar. Then I connect this scent with the sweet, salty smell already coating my hands. She catches my puzzlement and then smiles with certainty when she realizes I know the source of their shiny coat.

"You should get a lot of use out of them," she says. "Now you are one. One of the cult. The cunt cult."

The place before language

✦✦✦✦   *Lucy Jane Bledsoe*

Picture me in my Class-A National Park Service uniform:
the polished-to-a-luster shoes, the green trousers with
the razor-sharp crease, the belt with the embossed pine cones,
the short green jacket with the shiny badge and brass buttons,
and the wide-brimmed Smokey the Bear hat. The whole bit.
You see a woman who can name every wildflower on Mount
Rainier, who has climbed at least eight major peaks, who
knows the secret life of glaciers.

You think you see a woman in control.

You see a femme at heart hoping to find relief in a butch
getup.

You see me, a woman whose summer job as a ranger on
Mount Rainier had not stopped her raging fantasies about
murdering Donna's new girlfriend. Graphic pictures — of my
hands around her neck, of my green Park Service truck
colliding with her bulk — lit the dark recesses of my mind
like little nuclear explosions. I couldn't stop them. I didn't
want to.

She — the new girlfriend — was dog ugly and had a
personality that lurked in dark corners. She looked like she

needed a vigorous trot in country air. Near the end of our ten years together, Donna had called me a bulldozer, and compared to this beige, papery moth, I suppose I did come across forcefully. I never denied being a high-maintenance girlfriend. I knew I wasn't an easy person. But then I had trusted "easy" wasn't what Donna was after.

No, it wasn't my bright obsession with violence that disturbed me. If I'd had the chance to act on my fantasies, I don't doubt that I would have. What really bothered me was the feeling that my grasp on everything I'd always known to be true was slipping, that a vital part of my brain had shaken loose and was rattling around in my head like useless machinery. You see, until that summer, I had believed in the power of language. As a writer, I lived with the conviction that everything could be said. Words were life's cradle, the way to name, shape, hold, and, yes, control one's world. I had always believed that as I sharpened my verbal skills so too would my world view come more crisply into focus. Language to me was like a massive database where one filed away experience — relentlessly, day after day. Even as I was living each moment, I was assigning words to it, writing it, wrapping it up in a neat package of verbiage.

This word castle crumbled when Donna dumped me. Even my agent, whose job was to promote my words and who'd treated me like the next Willa Cather just a few months before, quit returning my phone calls, as if she'd been in cahoots with Donna. I felt hollow and formless when I started the summer on Mount Rainier. All I had were visions of human roadkill flaring up in my gut like a forest fire, hot and out of control. That and this uniform.

I was stationed for the summer at Sunrise, a set of cabins just above treeline on the east side of the mountain. When I arrived there in mid-June, a roommate had already moved in.

"I've taken the bottom bunk," she said, "but if you prefer it we can draw straws."

"I'm usually a bottom," I answered to amuse myself, "but I need a change. I'll take the top."

In those first couple weeks, I hardly used the bunk at all. I tried to work on short fiction in the evenings, but nothing ever came. I couldn't sleep, either, so I spent the nights haunting the trails around Sunrise. Up there the mountain was so close it filled up half the sky, and even when the moon wasn't out, the stars were so abundant and the mountain so bright with glaciers that I could go anywhere without a flashlight. I would climb out to the end of Sourdough Ridge or explore the Silver Forest, a shadowy grove of smooth silver snags left over from a fire long ago. The meadows were full of columbine, aster, paintbrush, phlox, heather, monkey-flower, and lupine, and where the snow was just melting, glacier lilies, their colors rich and magical in the starlight. Sometimes I would hike out to Frozen Lake or down to Sunrise Lake.

These night prowls provided no insights, no answers, no inspirations, and no relief from wanting to murder Lurking Dog. I felt eclipsed by the massive glowing mountain, as if I didn't exist at all against its commanding backdrop. And yet, looking back, I see that these hikes were a kind of boot camp of the soul. I was getting ready.

On the first of July, three kids turned up missing on the mountain. Two boys, seventeen and eighteen, and a girl, sixteen, had begun climbing Rainier the day before. They were expected back at the White River camp by late after-noon. They never arrived.

I'd seen the kids earlier in the day. The Sunrise visitor center has enormous glass windows facing the mountain, and from there climbers look like tiny strings of ants. With strong binoculars you can make out their ropes, ice axes, and wool caps. That morning I'd seen the three dots and had been impressed because they were climbing quickly — and also because no one should have been on the mountain. The clouds, full and still, were turning that polished gray color that means a storm is brewing. The Park Service had put out an advisory against climbing. The kids, according to their friends at the White River camp, had come all the way from Wisconsin to climb and they had to be home at the end of the week. They decided to take their chances.

By ten that night, Jack Keeney, the head backcountry ranger, was putting together a search-and-rescue party. Night had swept in around the mountain along with a stiff wind and spitting rain. Up there, it would be snow. I drank coffee in the visitor center with the rest of the interpretive staff and listened to Jack, who was next door in the ranger station on the shortwave radio, summoning as many climbers as he could find.

The voices on the radio were all men's save one. Elise Sawyer's. The Mount Fremont lookout, where Elise had been stationed every summer for the past ten years, was primarily a fire tower. But it was also positioned for relaying messages around to the other side of the mountain. I'd heard Jack say how Elise had never missed a single fire. She was more dependable than any man he knew. Most fire lookout people had been replaced by patrol planes. But as long as she wanted it, Jack had said, Elise Sawyer could have her job.

I remembered meeting both Elise and Jack a month before at the beginning-of-the-season cookout for summer employees. Elise had looked like the only prospective dyke in the crowd, so after getting my food, I followed her to the shade of a Douglas fir, where she joined a tall, auburn-haired woman and a man who looked like an army sergeant. Elise looked the man dead in the eye, without smiling, and shook his hand firmly, saying, "Jack. Good to see you." Only then did she turn to the woman and say, "How're you doing, Barbara?" All three of them ignored me. I could have left, but then I'd have to try to break into some other conversation. At least here I had the chance of meeting a dyke. So I introduced myself. Balancing my limp paper plate of ribs, corn on the cob, and green salad in one hand, I shook their hands with my other. Elise Sawyer was less than friendly, almost sulky, but I liked Barbara and Jack. Besides her bronze hair, Barbara had formidable cheekbones and a mouth that looked vulnerable, as if she were ready to kiss someone. Jack had a flattop crew cut, big dimples, and a lean, muscled body. Together they broadcast a feeling of capability, like they were a team more than a marriage. I imagined them having athletic sex.

As the conversation stumbled along, tensely I thought, I tried to make significant eye contact with Elise. She appeared not just disinterested in me, but almost hostile. I got the feeling she wanted Jack and Barbara to herself. Shit, I thought, I wasn't trying to flirt with her or anything. Could a little lesbian camaraderie hurt? I left to get more ribs, thinking that this was going to be an even lonelier summer than I had anticipated.

I had not spoken with Elise since those few words at the cookout a month before. Tonight her butchy voice on the radio stirred me. Her competence, her complete control of the situation impressed me. I wished I could help. But despite my extensive climbing experience, women were not considered for search-and-rescue teams.

I remained quiet as my fellow Park Service employees clucked and shook their heads at the reckless climbers. They'd wanted only to climb the mountain. They'd driven all the way from Wisconsin. They'd wanted it badly. I found myself respecting those kids, who'd ignored good judgment, and hating these folks around me, who doled out their lives like treats that had to last a long time. Good judgment suddenly felt as slippery as a trout in hand. Was death really a fair punishment for ignoring storm warnings?

I felt restless, so I went back to my cabin and pulled on a sweatshirt, my down parka, and my Gortex suit. I set out in the thick mist, treading the mile out to Frozen Lake where the trail forked in three directions. One went up to Burrough's Mountain, one down to Berkeley Park, and the third over to the lookout tower on Mount Fremont. I climbed in the opposite direction of the lookout tower. The dense clouds made the night black and cold. Patches of snow still nestled against the leeward slopes.

The frozen mist engulfed me until I reached the top of Burrough's Mountain, where I could climb out of it. I breathed hard, feeling utterly alone. But something was different tonight. My insignificance in the face of this immense universe pleased me. By abandoning good judgment, those three kids had been cut loose. They were free agents in the cosmos. As much as I worried about them, I also envied them. What did good judgment have to do with anything?

From where I stood I could see the lookout tower on Mount Fremont, glowing with a warm yellow light. I pictured Elise stationed at the radio, relaying flawless messages from Jack to Paradise on the west side of the mountain. I didn't plan to do what I did next. Shivering, I headed back down Burrough's Mountain, cold and tired and hungry, thinking I would go home to bed. Instead, when I got to the junction at Frozen Lake, I started up Mount Fremont. As I approached I could see Elise's silhouette in the all-glass room at the top of her tower. Though I was still a quarter of a mile away, Elise came out on the tiny balcony that surrounded her glass perch. They were right when they said she missed nothing from her tower. I didn't call out or wave. So what if she was frightened by the approach of someone in the dead of night. That's what she got for being unfriendly at the cookout.

When I got to the base of the tower neither of us had spoken yet. I was a bit disappointed to realize that she wasn't one bit scared. She looked annoyed. I climbed the stairs and met her on the balcony. She wore a red-and-gray flannel shirt over a white t-shirt and Levi's. Clearly Elise didn't relish my intrusion.

"Did Jack send you?" she asked gruffly.

"No. I went out for a walk and landed here. Can I come in?" I was surprised at how aggressive I was being. For a femme out of uniform, anyway.

She turned and entered her tiny room, leaving the door open. After I followed, she went back to shut the door and then filled a beat-up tin pan with water from a metal tank on the floor and put the pan on a propane burner.

"I won't bother you. I mean, I know you're relaying messages for Jack."

"The search-and-rescue party just left. They won't need me anymore," she said, fingering the radio. "They've got six climbers. They're hoping to make the top of the Inter Glacier by midnight. Another party is going up from the Paradise side. Apparently the kids had talked about maybe going down the west-side route and hitching back to White River."

Jack's voice came across the radio. It was fuzzy and distant, but I could pick up some of the words. "Bob, I want you to personally check the carabiners on each ... Then we'll..." His voice faded out again.

"Where'd you learn to use that thing?" I asked.

She stopped to listen to Jack and didn't answer me.

Besides the radio, her tower was equipped with a map table, a direction finder, and high-powered binoculars. Jack's voice faded in and out as I looked over her instruments and maps.

"Jack knows exactly what he's doing," she said. "There's never a spare word in his communication. It's always tight and to the point."

So this was a mutual admiration party of two. She spoke of Jack with so much veneration I began to wonder if I'd been wrong about her being a lesbian. Maybe she was one of those types that was nothing, neither straight nor lesbian. She *felt* lesbian to me, though. She definitely had dyke essence.

"Listen to him," Elise said, sitting down. She stirred instant-coffee crystals into two tin mugs. "He's perfect."

"That's a strong statement," I said, thinking about Jack's auburn-haired wife, the fire in her eyes. The way she stood next to perfect Jack, her fingers curled around his biceps.

Elise nodded absently. "Want chocolate in your coffee?"

"Sure."

"Are you hungry?"

I was very hungry and nodded.

Elise smiled. Oh, I felt as if I'd seen an endangered species. That rare smile melted the knot in my throat.

She opened a plastic bag of mixed dried fruit and put it on the map table. Then she put on another pot of water. "I'll make soup."

In response to my questions, Elise showed me how the direction finder worked. She pointed out where the biggest fires of her tenure had occurred and explained exactly how she'd spotted them and what techniques had been used to smother them. Until she hurt her back she'd been a smoke jumper for the forest service, a firefighter who jumped from helicopters into burns too deep in the wilderness to reach by foot or road vehicle. She told me about the black bear she'd known since it was a cub that visited her several times a summer. It had a brown spot on the right side of its nose and its paws were even more pigeon-toed than other black bears. This summer the bear had brought her own cubs for Elise to see. Tears came to Elise's eyes as she told me this. No, of course she hadn't named the bear. It was a bear, not a person. And of course she never fed her. It was cruel to teach bears to rely on people.

I had the feeling Elise thought it was cruel to teach *people* to rely on people.

Elise seemed a bit like a bear to me. She had that round, solid build and bright eyes. She contained her strength rather than strutting it. She also had a clean, direct way of talking that moved her stories straight to my heart. I hadn't expected her to be a talker, especially not to a middle-of-the-night intruder. But she seemed blasé about my unexpected arrival, as if she had visitors on many nights. After we'd drunk two cups of mocha each, she ladled chicken noodle soup into my cup, without rinsing it, and set a box of crackers next to me. She had a way of offering food that was both clumsy and tender. It made me feel shy about looking her in the eye. We didn't talk as we dunked crackers into the soup and slurped up the noodles.

From the tower all I could see was the black night, and yet the light shifted minute by minute as the clouds moved, thinned, and then thickened again. The hot drinks and our warm bodies heated the room and soon I was toasty.

"If you have to pee," she said, breaking the silence, "the outhouse is down the stairs and to the right."

I did. Outside, I felt something stir in the night and turned, half expecting the bear and her cubs. But it was something bigger. It was the wilderness itself stirring in my gut. When I returned, Elise was sitting on her cot where she'd been when I left. Her back was against one of the glass windows and her legs lay open, one along the side of the cot and the other hanging off the edge. Instead of sitting back down on the stool by the map table, I sat on the cot and leaned back against her leg. Neither of us spoke for a long time. I let my body sink more deeply into her cot, against her leg, settling so that I was more *between* her legs. She picked up the foot that was on the floor and moved her legs so that they loosely encircled me. Outside, the forest of green-black trees extended for hundreds of miles in one direction. In the other, Mount Rainier rumbled gently in the night, three kids lost in the clouds blanketing her flanks, hot molten lava gurgling in her heart. Again, I felt the wilderness seize me, as if she were a lover.

I was going to ask something about the bear and her cubs but Jack's voice came, suddenly clear, on the radio. "Camp Sherman, come in."

Another man's voice, small and tinny but still audible, replied, "Roger."

"Have you looked over the western ridge of Steamboat Prow? Over."

"Negative. But we have to turn back, Jack. It's snowing harder and harder. I can't risk the lives of the whole crew. Seeking permission to turn back. Over."

There was a long silence before Jack answered. Then, firmly, "Granted. Come on back. Over."

"Ten-four. We'll stay at Camp Sherman tonight and try again in the..."

The voices faded again.

"The kids haven't a chance," I whispered. "Not overnight."

"Maybe," Elise answered. "Sounds like the searchers are going to camp at eleven thousand feet and try again in the morning. People have survived nights on the mountain. Maybe it'll clear."

"Maybe," I agreed.

Elise reached up and pushed her fingers through my hair, starting at my neck and moving to the crown of my head. "I love curly hair," she said.

"Oh," I answered, surprised to hear her say something personal. She placed her other hand on my knee and pulled so that my legs were open. Then she traced the inseam of my jeans with her middle finger, moving from my knee up. "Your jeans are almost worn out," she said, touching the frayed places on my Levi's. Her hands were beautiful. They were strong and rough, the fingernails bitten.

I wished I could have answered with something just as casual, but I didn't trust my voice. The wind whistled across the roof of her tower. The windows shook. She scooted forward so that she was pressed against my hip and then she tightened the grip of her legs around me. I had never wanted anyone in my life as badly as I wanted this woman.

Her fingers moved gracefully as she undid the buttons of my shirt and pulled it off my shoulders. I sat on the cot in my worn Levi's and bra while she slipped onto her knees on the floor and unbuttoned my pants. I realized then that she wasn't even going to take off her boots.

I felt myself giving in to something dangerous, as if I were about to enter the mountain blizzard as foolishly willing as those three kids. I held myself back. I said, "I didn't come here for this." Elise didn't answer. Her strong hands tugged my jeans down over my hips. The voices on the radio scratched on and off as the steam on the windows of the glass walls sealed us in. I began to disappear into the hollow of my belly, somewhere much deeper than my own body.

Elise pushed me back on the cot and leaned down to take a nipple, through my bra, into her mouth. Her hands cradled my neck for a while, as if this were going to be very tender lovemaking. But soon she slid them across my collarbone, briefly gripping my shoulders, and then moving down my sides and over my hips. She handled me roughly now, as if she were desperate for the nourishment my breasts, belly, and thighs gave her. I struggled to stay in my body, but I could no more return from this journey than those kids could find their way down the mountain this stormy night. As I came the first time, my mind slipped away, disappeared altogether, and I found myself in a foreign land. It was like the universe, black with stars all around. It was like the top of the mountain, desolate and empty, yet all I could ever need. It was a land that predated all that I knew to be true. As if creation were happening all around me. In and through me.

Some time, I don't know how many orgasms later, I returned to the lookout tower. Elise was rocking between my legs, her fist still in me. My head hung so far off her cot it nearly touched the floor, but she had one arm securely behind my shoulders to keep it from bonking on the wooden planks. Seeing I had come back, she effortlessly lifted my head and shoulders onto the cot. I know I looked at her with uncompromised worship. "Don't," was all she said. And I knew she was right. It wasn't Elise, it was that land on the other side that had made me reverent.

Outside the sky had lightened. The tiny room smelled musky and hot. The back of my throat ached with desire, an aftertaste I knew would never go away. Elise cracked open the door to clear the windows. The clouds had fled and a scattering of stars still remained in the paling sky. I lay on the cot, not moving, and watched the mountain turn peach and then bright yellow as the sun rose. The storm had lifted. Could the kids still be alive?

I loved Elise for not saying "You better go," though she was already at her instruments, measuring wind speed and direction, reading her barometer, recording the morning's temperature, writing down the exact moment of sunrise.

Messages were singing across her radio. She seemed to ignore them until suddenly she pivoted and took up the radio. A voice was calling urgently, "Fremont, come in. Fremont, come in."

"This is Fremont. Go ahead." Elise was all business.

"We found 'em. One mile from Paradise." The voice paused. I heard a sharp exhale of breath. Then, "All three dead. Transmit to Jack and stand by. Over."

"Ten-four. Verify message for Jack: Three climbers found dead one mile from Paradise. Over."

"Ten-four. Over and out."

"Over and out."

Elise didn't even look at me. She called Jack. "Communication from the Paradise search-and-rescue: The three climbers were found dead one mile from Paradise. Over."

Jack was silent for a long time. "Shit," he said into the radio. Jack, who never broke a rule, yelled, "Shit, shit, *shit.*"

Elise waited. Then she spoke: "Jack, is there anything you want to relay? Over."

"Negative. Stand by. Over and out."

"Ten-four. Over and out."

I dressed quickly, then walked over and put a hand on Elise's shoulder. "I'm going now," I said. My hand was shaking.

"Okay, then." Elise stood up and put her hands in her front pockets. She looked me dead in the eye, as she had with Jack at the cookout. I felt inadequate in the face of that look. I knew my own eyes swam with sleeplessness and utter fulfillment, that my hair was foolishly smashed to one side.

"The kids," I said. I wanted to cry so badly.

Elise nodded.

They only wanted to climb the mountain. They came all the way from Wisconsin. I left, running down the wooden stairs of her tower, crying hard as I jogged the five miles to my cabin at Sunrise.

◆◆◆◆

I couldn't think of anything but the three dead teenagers. And Elise. Night after night, I kept myself from stalking back out to her lookout tower. I tried to use up my energy by running out to the end of Sourdough Ridge and roaming through the Silver Forest. One night I even swam at midnight in Sunrise Lake, stroking through the black and icy glacial water. The lake was deep, and at the bottom lay a thick mud where all kinds of slimy worms and crustaceans lived. I flipped over on my back and floated, touching myself and thinking of Elise. Even that ice water wouldn't put out the fire she'd lit in me.

Donna and Lurking Dog — as well as my visions of homicide — became ancient and vague memories. Thank God Donna left me, I found myself thinking, so that I could be here for this. Even the anxiety that my pool of stories had dried up, that I'd never write again, disappeared. What did stories matter when I thought about those three dead teenagers? When I thought of Elise? Everything had become unbearably immediate.

And yet, as badly as I wanted her, I knew that to return to Elise would be to miss the point. The coordinates of time and space had brought us together for a moment, and it was this coincidence that made it work for her, maybe even for me. I should let that moment explode like a star, hot and bright, a thing unto itself. But I couldn't. I wanted to be touched by her calloused hands again. I wanted to see her dark brown eyes that looked like soil, like hard work. I wanted to touch her strong back and feel her skilled strength deliver me outside of myself. On the seventh night, I tracked back out there, moving like a shadow. My plan was to stop at a distance and only watch her. If I was lucky she'd be up with her lantern lit.

As I approached I saw that her lantern was indeed lit. I scuttled along the trail, keeping my eyes lowered so I wouldn't attract her attention, and ducked behind a large boulder about a hundred yards from the tower. I was breathing hard and was afraid she'd already detected my presence. Slowly, I eased my head around the side of the boulder to look.

There was someone in the tower with Elise. Two women were silhouetted against the night. One woman had her hands braced behind her, on what would be Elise's map table, her head thrown back. My view gave me a perfect profile and I could see the woman's open mouth and her hair hanging freely behind her head. Her breasts lifted up toward the ceiling of the tower. Another head was between her legs. "Sweet Jesus," I murmured, sinking back behind the boulder.

The moon was bigger now than it'd been the week before, and it cast long shadows. The brightness of the mountain made it feel like daylight out here. I shifted my weight and an old piece of wood cracked, sounding like an explosion in the stillness of the night. I froze. I counted to ten. Then I slid my head around the rock again to see if I'd caught their attention. Hardly. Elise's head was still decidedly between the woman's legs. She stayed like that for what seemed like hours, the other woman's mouth opening and closing in what appeared to be gasps, her hips rocking back and forth in Elise's hands.

Finally, the woman pulled Elise up by her collar and they sunk into a long kiss, the woman lying back on the map table now and Elise pressing on top. After awhile the stranger pushed Elise off of her and reached for something on the floor. Her shirt. Elise helped her get her arms in it and then tenderly buttoned it up for her. With me, Elise hadn't been so much tender as she'd been deft. Even at this distance I could see that Elise became malleable in the presence of this other woman.

The woman moved quickly now, as if she were late. She pulled on her jacket, kissed Elise again, and hurried out of the glass room and down the stairs of the tower. Shit! I hadn't thought about being discovered by the stranger! There was no way I could escape without being seen. I had to wait behind the boulder and pray she would not see me as she passed on the trail just three yards away. I watched the woman approach. She hadn't come very far along the trail when I recognized Jack Keeney's wife, Barbara. Sweet Jesus! What was going on here?

I pressed myself against the back of the boulder, held my breath, and watched her half-run past me on the trail. She looked beautiful. Her hair bright in the moonlight, her gait loose and easy. When she was out of sight, I looked back at the tower.

I couldn't help myself. I waited a respectable amount of time and then stepped out from behind my rock and headed up to the fire tower. For once, Elise wasn't aware of everything that came within a hundred yards. As I approached I saw her blow out her lantern. I drew close.

I still couldn't believe what I'd seen. All I'd ever heard from the other rangers was how much they envied Jack and Barbara's marriage. They shared so much together: a love of the outdoors, a clear decision not to have children, a simple close-to-the-bone existence. Barbara, I'd heard from the male rangers, was the perfect woman, both gorgeous and able to keep up. I just couldn't believe this. And the way Elise nearly worshipped Jack. Her boss.

I started up the stairs. My footsteps echoing on the lumber must have startled her. She called out, "Barbara?" She thought her lover had returned.

She had, but not the one she expected.

"Barbara!" This time her voice was urgent.

I paused a moment. Then I called out, "It's me."

Elise appeared at her door in her long underwear. She looked softer than I'd ever seen her. I wanted her more than ever. But a vulnerable butch is something you don't mess with. I stopped my approach, like an animal who understands territory. She was literally speechless.

I said, "I saw everything." Trying to lighten the mood, I added, "So how many women traipse out here for your services, anyway? I thought your job was putting *out* fires."

Elise looked me over good and long, still speechless and maybe even frightened. She knew next to nothing about me, and I had first-class blackmail information on her.

"Can I come in?"

She stepped out of the doorway and let me in.

Elise had been crying. I noticed the wet patch on her pillow, the red blotches on her face, her eyelashes clumped together with tears. I stood awkwardly next to the map table, not knowing what to do but unwilling to leave.

She suddenly began sobbing. "I don't cry," she forced out between sobs. "I don't cry in front of people."

"You are now," I said softly. "You are now."

I filled her tin pan with water from the tank. Then I fiddled around trying to light her propane burner, which provided her with the opportunity to get up, push me aside, and do it herself. That helped. She paced for a while, looking more like a bear than ever.

"Ten years this year," she began, wiping her nose on her sleeve. "Barbara and I have been lovers for ten years, ever since my first summer up here." She laughed hoarsely and ran her hands through her short hair. "Oh, we've broken it off a million times, sometimes me and sometimes her. One summer we made it through the whole season without having sex once."

"Why doesn't she leave Jack?"

Elise looked at me as if I were crazy. "Jack doesn't have anything to do with it."

It seemed to me that Jack would have everything to do with it. "Does he know?"

"Of course not. But they have a perfect relationship. Jack ... Jack, he's..." For a moment Elise seemed at a loss for words. Then, "Jack is so solid. No woman in her right mind would ever leave Jack. You know, he was a POW in Vietnam. He's the kind of person that every year you know him you learn more. I love Barbara too much to ever want her to leave Jack. Ever." Elise was almost growling now.

After a long silence, she whispered huskily, "But..."

I waited.

"But every time she leaves me it's harder. Every single year it gets wilder, bigger, deeper." She turned off the boiling water and started to make coffee. "I spend every winter ravaging women at home in Michigan, looking for one who can call up the passion Barbara calls up in me. But Barbara, she's this rock in my heart." Elise was fierce. "Do you understand?"

I nodded. I thought I did. I wondered how many of those ravaged women in Michigan felt as awed by Elise as I did now.

"You're the only person I've ever told."

"I swear I'll never breathe a word to anyone."

Elise smiled softly, nodded a little.

I waited for her to say something more, but she was quiet. She made only one cup of coffee. I could tell she wanted to be alone. I was no replacement for Barbara. I stood to go.

"You know, Elise," I said, "you're about the best thing I've come across in my whole life."

She looked startled, ready to fend me off.

"Don't worry," I said and glanced out of her glass tower at the clean, bare surface of the nearly full moon. Something inside me rocketed past the ache at the back of my throat to that starry wilderness she'd shown me. It was the place before language. The place where all stories come from. Where life comes from.

I said, "You've made me hungry for myself."

The kissing booth

✦✦✦✦ *Debra Moskowitz*

Somehow I'd been roped into volunteering an hour at the kissing booth. It was a women-only benefit for the Women's Center building fund, back in the days when the objections to a kissing booth focused on the exploitation of women, not on communicable diseases.

My friends had all paid a dollar to kiss me, as I'd made them promise they would, because I didn't want to show an empty till at the end of my shift. Actually, I hadn't done too badly with women I didn't know, either. With ten minutes left of my hour I counted seventeen dollars in the little metal cashbox on the table to my right. Dana was hanging around for moral support, and I looked up from counting when I heard her laugh. She was pointing into the palm of her hand, which she held up in front of her chest, giving me a hidden signal indicating there was someone behind her she wanted me to see. "The femme, the femme," she whispered, laughing.

I looked over and saw the femme half of the butch-femme couple we'd always found so amusing. I don't think I'd ever seen her alone before. She stood out in the crowd, a bit older than most of the women, her light brown hair pinned up on top of her head in a loose Gibson Girl style. A long, frilly pink dress with a tiny floral print covered her soft, slightly plump body. It wasn't even a hippie dress, which was about all you could get away with back then. And she wore matching pink lipstick when absolutely no one else, lesbian, bi, or straight, was even wearing eye makeup. There was hardly a woman there in anything but jeans.

Dana turned around to take another look, turned back to me with her hand over her mouth, and moved off to the side. The femme was heading right toward me. I looked down at the table to avoid any eye contact that might invite her over, but when I picked my head up she was standing in front of me, gazing directly at me, or as directly as she could. Her left eye drifted slightly inward, which kept me from being sure exactly what she was looking at. She extended a crisp dollar bill toward me.

"Hello," I said and smiled. I'd never spoken to her before. She flashed her cross-eyed smile and said nothing. Over in the corner of the room, Dana had grabbed Robin, and they were laughing so hard I saw Robin drop to the floor.

I took the dollar bill, put it in the cashbox, and stood up. I smiled again but my lips were too dry to make the stretch, so I licked them, and as I leaned forward to kiss the femme, she murmured under her breath, "That's right, honey, get those lips nice and wet for me."

Oh, wait till the girls hear this one, I thought. Yet I found that my heart was beating a bit too fast. My friends, and the other women who'd paid their dollar to kiss me, had all given me playful, mostly dry, pecks. But the femme was a bar dyke, and I wondered if she knew the unspoken rules of the game at the Women's Center.

She was about four inches shorter than me, so I bent down, conscious of Robin and Dana watching from across the room.

And then her lips covered mine, and she opened one hand flat against the side of my face; her other hand gripped my biceps with surprisingly strong fingers, painted nails biting slightly into the flesh under my upper arm. She drew me down closer to her than I'd planned on being, our breasts not quite touching but near enough so I could feel the heat of her. The hand on my face held firm; she kissed me with short staccato strokes, wet and open-mouthed but all lips, no tongue. Kiss release, kiss release. I felt my mouth open to hers and I tried to pull away to catch my breath between kisses, but I couldn't get enough air to fight the dizziness that was beginning to weaken my legs. Her mouth was so sweet and so sure. She kissed each of my lips separately, gently pulling the top one into her mouth, and then the bottom one, and then her whole mouth was on mine again, open, wet heat, hot breath. I reached out and grabbed her shoulder to steady myself. I closed my eyes and all I knew was that kiss release, kiss release. The hand on the side of my face slid around to the back of my head, and as she ground her lips harder into mine, our teeth clicked. I tried to pull away, but she held the back of my head firmly and tightened her grip on my arm. She sucked my mouth into hers. I felt her tongue make a maddening, fleeting pass over mine, and then I felt pain in my bottom lip. A bite? An accident of teeth against flesh? I couldn't be sure. I couldn't even breathe. And then the kissing stopped, and she released my head so suddenly it jerked back as I pulled against the ghost of her hand.

"I guess that's about my dollar's worth," she said. Slowly, deliberately, she loosened her grip on my arm as I took in the surroundings I wasn't aware I'd lost. I drew a deep breath — air at last — and unconsciously sucked on my lower lip.

"Don't go wetting those lips again, sweetheart. I don't have any singles left," she teased. I opened my mouth to say something but just stood dumb, chest still heaving, pulse finally beginning to slow a bit. Her eyes were fascinating. I could see now that the cast was quite charming, almost beautiful.

When I looked up I saw that Dana and Robin had worked their way over to us and had moved in behind her, pretending to be next on line. Please let her walk off without seeing them laugh at her, I prayed.

She nodded good-bye to me and turned around to face them. "Worth a whole lot more than dollar, girls. Be gentle with her, now," she said as she picked up her purse and walked away.

"Oooooeee," Dana hooted. "Worth a whole lot more than a dollar." And then she leaned closer and squinted at me. "Is that lipstick on the side of your mouth?" she asked, wiping my cheek with her finger.

"Hey, let's start an auction for Hot Lips, and we'll pay off the mortgage tonight," said Robin.

"Cut it out, you guys," I said and they thought it was just embarrassment talking. But I was fighting to stay with that kiss, to keep that stir swirling from my belly to my breasts. I had to pull out of it before they guessed how badly she'd gotten to me. My shift was done. I turned the money box over to the woman in charge and walked off, my friends still teasing me.

"That was some long kiss," said Dana. "What the hell was going on there?"

"When the butch is away, the femme will play," Robin chanted.

"Well, come on, let's go to the bar," said Dana.

"You are still coming with us, aren't you, Hot Lips?" Robin asked.

I turned and looked around the Women's Center. I saw the back of her pink flowered dress across the room, and I started toward her.

Emilee begins to learn

++++

Mia Levesque

At nineteen, fearing the eternal agony of my virginity, I made my decision. Although my objectives were clear, the methods remained blurred, obscured by societal dictation and expectation. I was alone in my life, alone in my decision, and I would live by my own judgment. I did not choose my fate, but I chose from the paths that were laid before me.

++++

I go by bus, getting off when I know that I have arrived. As I anticipated, I am virtually alone in the stark Sunday morning light. And I wait, knowing I can leave at any moment. I wait. I have waited, romanticizing about love...

Romance may have motivated the princess to converse with the frog, but lust forged that fateful kiss. No one ever teaches a woman to search; they only tell her to wait for that lustful prince to hypnotize her with the delusion of love. There are no princes from where I stand, only frogs. I am like any princess who must use a frog to try to learn to be a prince.

At nineteen I want a princess; I find a prostitute.

I stand on the corner, waiting to be approached. No one comes, so I approach, ask around, try to find someone willing to "do girls." I suddenly feel young, inexperienced, and very female. When she finally approaches, she is taller and not much older.

What do you want, baby?

She is checking me out, looking me up and down. I am an unlikely suspect, I realize. I seem like a country girl, like I drove in from middle-of-nowhere America. So I do not fit the image, but then neither does she. I expected less, wanted more.

What can I do for you, girlie-girl? You looking for your mama or shopping for your big brother?

I think I am looking for a fuck, not a fuck-over. I don't say this. My mind remains uninhibited, but somewhere along their journey, the forceful, protective words always lose their nerve, doubt themselves, and become once again timid. So I just stand there, a dumb, expressionless look on my sun-tinted face.

I want to ... buy ... damn ... I have enough...

Oh, baby, don't get all flustered. Let's go. I'll take care of you.

I follow her into the room. I am scared, but I show no fear. I ask no questions, only wait to begin. She gives no answers, only waits to finish. She will sacrifice me. I know of no other way. Sexual knowledge is the gift of experience. In return for that gift, an offering is expected. I prepay.

I want to be alone, to escape into my forbidden world, that which is me, selfish and introverted, at peace in my solitude and with the familiarity of my loneliness. But she is here, removing her coat. I want seduction; I get sex.

How do you want it, she says.

I don't know. No one has ever physically been there except me. So I reach deep into the soul, reach back into the recesses of repressed, undesirable female emotion. I find lust. I am afraid of the collapse of my solar plexus, lost in what seems to be a moment free from time. How do I want it? I want it slow, complete; I want passion, and I need silence. Words break the anonymity. I don't want to think or hear. Am I the one in control? Somehow I expect that I should be. It feels unnatural. I am not the man, the john, but I am.

The room is green; the bedspread has large gold flowers. The smell is musty, damp; it lacks sunlight or warmth. I want it slow, one button at time, one long second at a time. Standing, I watch, stare, gawk. One shoulder at a time, sleeves off, shirt gone. Black bra. My back is weak, my breath warm and fast. I don't know her, but I want her. Skirt unzipped, it drops easily to the floor. Bra and garter belt. I realize that I have never seen a living, breathing naked woman. If ever I had the opportunity, I turned away, confused by shyness and anxiety, afraid that I was doing something wrong but was unaware of the rules. She senses my naiveté, my innocence, my inability to move. Her amber hair almost touches her shoulders and rests against her face. Time elapses and I touch her. I will cease to exist, explode, evaporate. Her hair is soft and unkempt; her shoulders are smooth, caramel in color.

I pull at her bra. I am inept. In frustration I back away, but she is professional. She follows me, removing her bra as she approaches. She walks me through what I feel I should somehow already know. She places my hand on her breast. With my shirt removed, I feel the air on my naked back, although I am too numb to feel if it is hot or cold. Fear becomes wet and dissolves — one hook, one button, one zipper. Sliding down my hips, black jeans. One push and I am down, flat on my back, feeling the lumps and disfigurement of an old, abused mattress. Her simplest touch is stronger than any self-induced orgasm. Stockings undone, sliding off each leg. Against the warmth of my flesh, her cold hands find my inner thighs. I am nineteen; I am spread ... exposed. This is raw. Breast to breast, this is sex.

Blank mind, taste of salt from the sweat dripping slowly down my cheek and into my parted mouth. Have I passed out? No, because the taste is so real. She toys with me, pushing my legs farther and farther apart. Hands between my legs glide down behind my knees, lift my legs in the air. She thrusts inches from my crotch. I want to pull myself to her, but she makes me wait, makes me sweat. I feel every move so intensely that I am acutely conscious of only one sense at each moment. Rotate, slide, hide, I am blind. My thighs ache, stretched out before the world. Focus on the ceiling, my eyes wide, and suddenly I see. White, gray, cracked, I am deaf. Tight pain, she is inside me. One finger at a time, she comes inside, latex glove pushing in, pulling out. I widen. Pleasure pain, or so they say, those who create the image of sex for the yet inexperienced, and this is what they meant. Dank, humid, drenched, I smell. I am sweet, honey for the bees, wet. Her lips fade below, find the crevice of my hip. My lips want to kiss her. Mouth moving against my thigh. She has soaked me. Engulf me; milk and honey, swallow me. But she will not; no rubber ... damn ... to stop my flood.

I am acutely aware of the weight of my own body, as I lie flat on my back. My arms are heavy in the surrounding space. This is about feeling more than alone. Beyond thinking, my weight takes over. I want to feel it all, every move, but how can my body wait? I can't wait to feel her weight. Her lips hover between my legs. Not this time, she says, but she knows that this is just beginning. Three fingers pushed inside. Taut, smooth, wide, I can't hide. Drops dripping down, sliding in grooves, coating, still spread, wet ass. And as her thumb rubs against me, holds and presses my clit, her still inside, I don't wait. I want to feel her weight. My senses are restored; my mind is blank, my body weak and fatigued. I feel the seemingly endless aftershocks between my legs, down my thighs, over my hips.

◆◆◆◆

Virginity lost, I left. She was unfulfilled, but I would see her again. I knew. And as I stepped into the cold, for a brief moment the sun warmed my sadness. Still, the tears froze upon my face. In my dreams, she would come — all over me. She would thrust and grind. In my dreams, I was never wet; I remained unaffected. Controlled. Then, I would wake up, sheets wet, and would relieve myself. Again, I felt that I had lost, but I was learning.

At night I used to think: I want to get laid. I would think sex, raw, bold, without emotional commitment. I wanted physical contact, brief attraction, all the buildup with limited disappointment. I wanted to know exactly what I was getting. I wanted to be accustomed, to not expect that which was not. We would fuck for the painstakingly honest need to fuck. I would not expect more and would leave with only mild distaste for my actions, the crumpled piece of scrap paper with a phone number scrawled on it clenched tightly in my sweaty palm. I would be no better yet no worse for having "known" her. But this would not fool me. I would rather leave with less money, little illusion, and few pretenses. I quested for a teacher, not a playmate. Fuck me, don't fuck me over. So now I went straight to the streets instead of a bar. I figured that, considering the cost of drinks, I broke even financially. Emotionally, everything was probably comparable as well; however, physically, I craved more. I returned.

The second time I went to see her, I was not yet sure what to expect. What did I want? Images of sex rushed through my conscience. I could not forget. Still I knew that I wanted more. I waited on the same corner, hoping. This time, the rain poured down, covering.

✦✦✦✦

Sunday morning in the rain is not the same as any other morning. This time, I see the street, the corner, the metal sheets pulled down over the fronts of store windows, windows sleeping. I smell the wet morning gutter. I gaze at myself in the naked window of an aged flower shop. I am about image. My black motorcycle boots, my silver rings on every finger of my left hand including my thumb, my loose-fit jeans. I am about image, my right ear pierced three times. I wonder what I am trying to prove. I think that if she could fall, it would be for my motorcycle boots, maybe the way that the black leather has softened against the heat of my throbbing, nervous feet, pressed against the early spring pavement, steam rising from the scorched, wet street.

She is there. Crotch throbbing, heart pounding, rain-drenched, I wait for her to approach. I feel natural in the oddity of my waiting on the street corner. She sees me and approaches. I want her without realizing my illusions. We return to the same hotel, different room, same room. She is here, with me. I am abstract in my desire. My romantic fantasy lives, beaten but unwilling to die. Through my thoughts, time passes, shirt sliding off soft shoulders, her breasts, naked, slip into my mouth; I am hungry. Her nipple hardens, my lips separate, my tongue circles. I am less intimidated this time. Still, I am shy and unsure of my skills. Concern for her pleasure exists, although the rules seem to say that it shouldn't. Sex between women is not inherently equal or well balanced. Some strange theory suggests that a woman always knows exactly what another woman wants. It isn't that simple. I don't know what she wants. Maybe she no longer wants anything from this act, this animal game, natural need, human desire. I want more than the sex, but everything blurs into one. When I reach between her legs, she is wet, adding to my confusion. Does she want me? At the time, I believed that she did. Say that you want me. I need someone to want me. I try to kiss her, to press my lips hard against hers, but she has other plans.

Well, this time, babe, I came prepared, no pun intended.

And she lowers herself down my body, hesitating, pausing, in her exploration. She takes in my salt as she tastes every curve. Slowly removing my opened shirt, she surrounds my breasts and reaches between my thighs. Sliding, mouth open, closing in on my stomach, I am breathing hard, too fast. Raise my hips toward her hand, I want her fingers between my lips; inside, I want her to grab handfuls of me, scoop me into her mouth. Still, she takes her time, moves slowly, just like I thought I wanted her to. Now the anticipation seems unbearable.

She kisses me with my legs spread open, touches me with her tongue pressed against the thin rubber wall. I feel all the pressure of my thick stream pushing against the dam. I imagine that the stream from her mouth meets with mine, and I feel her moistened lips parted against my lips. Her tongue still there, just beyond the barricade, talks to me, tells me a secret as it moves. Her hands are still gliding between my thighs, then up my hips, sliding to my waiting, hoping breasts. And this is all I can take as I reach for her face and come to her. I cum to her. So when I wake up, she is still there, sitting on the disheveled bouquet of gold flowers. I reach for her, once again touch her smooth body. I fumble between her legs as I pull myself around her and take her breast in my mouth. I am like an infant, and she knows this. I try to move my mouth down her waist.

Not this time, baby. You're gonna have to wait...

As she gets up to hook her garter belt, I know that again there will be a next time, because I am just beginning to learn.

Innocent lust

◆◆◆◆ *Nice Rodriguez*

On the day before I migrated to Canada, I knew there was something else I had to do. I had packed my bags, two nylon suitcases weighing 35 kilos each, containing a little of everything I owned for thirty years. I could not bring more in excess baggage for I only had $400 to live on until I found a job in Toronto.

I had spent the past days figuring out what to bring and not. What I could live without and what not. In the end, I realized it was my lover whom I wanted to pack with me to Canada.

In the Philippines, it was difficult to leave for abroad. Most embassies would not issue a traveling visa to any Filipino until they were sure he would return home. Many sought the greener pastures abroad, refusing to come back to a country of poverty, crime, violence, and injustice. Ironically, many escapees also became willing victims to the same atrocities in another land.

My lover had applied as an independent immigrant to Canada, but she could not get through. I was just lucky and tomorrow I must depart. Although her heart would weep, I knew she would send me off warmly. A Filipino never grieved for another one who must go away to escape the political turmoil in our country. No explanation was necessary. It was a common suffering which many of us sought to get away from someday. Tomorrow, it would be my turn.

My lover and I had lived together for three years, but I knew she must selflessly let me go. There was no other option. We both wanted to see the world that our parents and ancestors never saw, and earn the dollars they never made in their lifetimes. My mother and brother pooled their resources together for my fare and pocket money. My father offered beer for my *despedida*, a farewell party. Friends embraced and kissed me like they would never see me again. I felt like a tourist trapped in an immigrant's body. I just wanted a holiday but everybody was driving me away. It became clear they did not want me back and that my mission was to clear the way for them when their own departure came.

My immigration papers were ready. I had to say good-bye to more friends. I had had devastating affairs with two straight women before and both separations had been disheartening. I could not call them up for they would not care. Besides, if my lover found out, she would think I was being silly. I had been faithful to her all these years and I did not want her to worry now that I was going away. I crossed out their names.

There was one person to call on my list. She had not been a lover and we were never intimate. Thinking about her still sparks an arousal in me. I never knew what she felt about me. At that time, only my eyes revealed my lesbian spirit and very few people could read eyes.

We went to a Catholic high school in Manila that believed in the segregation of boys and girls. The nuns handled us girls. At that time, I felt more like a boy but had to go through lessons on crocheting, embroidery, needlework, and weaving.

I brought my projects home for my mom to finish. I wished the nuns would let me work in the boys' room — woodworking, drafting, mechanics, and leatherwork.

But segregation was the rule. We could not even mix with the boys who came in the afternoons. Just before they arrived, we must be out of the classrooms which we occupied in the mornings. Before they started classes, we girls must hurry down the stairs. Some wore shorts underneath our pleated blue skirts, fearing the boys who peeped through the slits between the stairs below would see our panties. My classmates never knew that sometimes I also sneaked a look at their underskirts. Well, there was really not much to see. Mainly legs and dark crotches.

Gigi, the person I wanted to call, joined our class late in high school. The other girls and I had been classmates for almost a decade now, some since our kindergarten days. Suddenly, a beautiful stranger appeared in our class. Nobody gave a damn except me.

The wide-open windows brought cool air but I perspired profusely. She freshened the air with an enchanting aroma I had never breathed before. Her nearness made me shiver. She came from an elite Catholic girls' school. She was slightly older, just a year or two maybe.

Each time I looked at her, I felt a surge of innocent lust. She had skinny arms but had a fully developed figure. We wore thin polyester white blouses and the nuns wanted us to wear chemises over our bras. Gigi was not wearing a chemise. Just a bra which I wanted to unhook at that time. Suddenly, this intruder filled the fantasies I had vented on my female teachers.

In the classrooms, the teachers grouped us alphabetically, but outdoors we lined up by height. I was almost as tall as she was so she was never far from me.

Soon I was telling her jokes which she liked a lot. It was not hard for I was a natural clown. With her, however, I always felt I was running out of gags. I did not call her Gigi but I christened her Kiki, which in Filipino means vagina. She endeared herself to me and I called her Ki. Soon others called her the same name but she did not mind being called Vagina. She had a game soul.

Her thick, black hair had a natural curl which I liked to roll around my young lesbian finger. She often enticed me with her round brown eyes and I would turn to stone. Her cheeks had a pinkish glow, and her lips were full and inviting. I wanted to kiss her but I was afraid.

I felt her force inside me. She was in my mind at school and at home. Not since her arrival had I worn such flawlessly shining shoes. I mended the holes in my socks and put elastics on them so they would not drop to my ankles for I thought that one day I might remove my shoes, maybe my clothes, in her presence. I saved money and went to the salon for haircuts. I asked my cousin to check my hair for dandruff and lice which I might have picked up over the summer. The more I thought about her, the more I felt inadequate.

Sometimes, I called Ki over the phone for all the wrong reasons — assignments, projects, boys — but never about what I felt for her. Soon I became her confidante.

She told me her parents were separated. In the Philippines, there was no divorce. Kids who were illegitimate and came from broken homes bore stigmas on them. It was easier to say that her dad had died but she told me her mother was living with someone else. I liked her candor.

I wanted to bang down the phone whenever she spoke of boys. We had given code names to most of the senior boys in school. She was in love with Milky Way. I knew her before Milky Way even courted her but he was a boy, and so had the right to say his feelings. I kept my lesbian yearnings to myself. At night, I caressed my pillow and cried her name.

I felt bad but Ki would still find time for me. We would do silly things like walk to Quirino Avenue where Milky Way lived just to look at his house where Ki said she would live someday. Below the mercury street lamps, we waited for a jeepney to board home. It was rush hour and it was nighttime before we got a ride.

"If I got a car someday, would you ride with me?" I asked her wistfully. Only the rich had cars back home and we were not rich. Milky Way had a car.

"Of course," she said. "Fetch me."

"Yes, I will," I said.

Sometimes Ki would come so close to me, brushing a breast on my elbow. It was hard to say if it was a signal since my other classmates also did the same. There were just too many breasts in the classroom, 112 of them since we were 56 girls cramped in a class. Since it was our lone intimate contact, I taught my elbows to be tender with Ki's breasts. Maybe she liked it too, I thought.

Other times, pretending to study, she would put my head between her thighs while she sat on the wooden school chair.

"Come here," she would call me. "Come to Mama."

I never knew what she meant but I came to her. Her legs were warm and I laid my head on her crotch. She touched my hair as she read her own book. I wanted to bury my head deeper into her.

The wooden chairs in the classrooms harbored bedbugs, and at times Ki would raise her skirt and show me the bite marks under her thighs. Sometimes, she lifted her skirt higher and I would blush. She never wore shorts. I blushed easily in her presence and she once wondered why I would get so red. I told her it could be a Vitamin B deficiency.

Until graduation day, I waited for the day Ki would stop talking about boys but she never did. If she had I would have dared confess my feelings even if it meant being expelled from school if the nuns found out. After a long wait, I figured out we were not meant for each other.

Besides, I was a neophyte. Even if I told Ki I loved her, I would not know what to do next.

How do lesbians make love? Honestly, at fifteen, I did not know. All the fiery sex manuals I read were about hetero-sexual exploits. What about same-sex erotica? There was none I could check back home. A Catholic country, these kind of books were probably set afire by religious groups. Maybe the priests and nuns kept it for their own reference. I was a scholarly nerd back then. Every answer I needed I sought in books.

As I got older, I learned it was mainly instinct — that when confronted with a nude female, I naturally knew what to do next. It was only in Canada, at age thirty, that I got to read lesbian erotica. As an adolescent, I read heterosexual books and so fantasized about having a cock and a hard-on. The illusion was so strong I even dreamed about having a sex transplant someday.

There were only two sexes in the Philippines. No institu-tion ever recognized the third sex. Since I could not be myself, I must believe I was a man. I told friends that I would save lots of money to get myself the biggest cock transplant ever.

Ki and I parted ways. In my graduation dress, I looked more queer than ever. Ki was radiant and the boys adored her. Soon she was dating the commanding officer of the school's military unit.

Two years later, she visited me at home. She was still a joy to behold with her easy laughter. She asked me to help her with her term paper. She said her boyfriend showed her his penis. She took my pen and paper and drew a cock for me.

"You forgot the veins," I said wryly. Ki made varicose details on her artwork. I had enough of her but could never turn her away. I told her to come back the next day for her term paper.

I saw her again after three years. At that time, I had moved out of the city to an east end suburb. I was then living with a lady from my newspaper's advertising department, who had a five-year-old son. I had a family. I saw Ki in my basement apartment in the city which I kept for convenience. The place was dusty and in disarray. Ki remembered my birthday and gave me a man's cologne.

Every object she touched would send dust off into the air and soon our hands and faces were smudged with dirt. It was hardly romantic. We laughed. She had flunked the government tests that I had passed the year before and we laughed again at her misfortune.

"I have done many things with men," she confessed, "but I'm still a virgin."

"You see, I have never done it with a man," I smiled. "I've done many silly things with women and I'm still a virgin."

We laughed even more. That was the last time I saw her.

◆◆◆◆

Several years passed and now that I was leaving, I remembered her again. I called up Ki at the local beer company where she worked.

"Ki, I'm going to Canada," I told her. "I wanted to say good-bye."

"But you can't go without seeing me," she demanded.

"I'm leaving tomorrow," I said. "Silly that I should call only now but I've got no time."

"I'm married now. I have a kid."

"Finally found someone," I said. "Well, I just wanted to tell you I was leaving."

"Okay," she said. "I will write. Take care."

And so I left. When I arrived in Toronto, I wrote Ki. It was the distance that gave me the courage to reveal what had long been unsaid.

> Dear Ki,
> I wanted you to know I loved you back then. Not in years had I found anything like it. I loved you more than Milky Way could ever have. I was afraid to ask — afraid for both of us.
> Love, N

The holidays approached and she mailed me a card.

> Dear N,
> I knew. Merry Christmas.
> Love, Ki, married with two kids.

It was a strange reply but I sighed with relief. After fifteen years, I could not believe I finally told Ki what I thought I could keep forever. She knew at last and I eventually put my lesbian longing to rest.

Filth

◆◆◆◆   *Karne Cutter*

Arriving early for work, Kim and I use our time as we always do: we drink our coffees, eat our bagels, and gossip about our co-workers. I believe most of what people tell me. I've been called gullible more than once. But sometimes I just don't buy a juicy tidbit, and it drives Kim nuts. She really does believe everything she hears.

"And you actually think this happened?" I ask Kim, trying to control the smirk forming on my lips.

"Why not?" I stare at her, amazed at her naïveté, her trust. "Listen, you've been there, you know the house." She pauses to let her reasoning sink in. "Think about it. I'm surprised it hasn't happened before."

◆◆◆◆

Kim has a point. I *have* been there, I *do* know the house. And I am *still* uncomfortable cleaning the bedroom. The house in question is actually a condo, situated in the economically depressed area of Cambridge's Central Square. I've never met the owner of the place, but every week I, or someone else from our cleaning company, go and spend an hour running a dust cloth over her furniture.

I work for a company called Cleaning Works. I show up at eight each weekday morning, get assigned to a three-person team, and go off to conquer the world's grime — or at least four or five households' worth. I like my job. I've been here a year and a half, longer than I ever imagined staying. The pay isn't good, but the dress is casual and days tend to be short — rarely do I work past three o'clock. There's a core group of about eighteen workers, about half of whom are lesbians. The others are Hispanic or Haitian, newly immigrated, not knowing English well, and working the only jobs open to them. I don't think they know what to make of all the short-haired, Levi's-clad girls they work with.

The woman who owns the condo in Central Square is a dyke. I knew that five minutes into my first visit. You learn a lot about a person by what appliances she owns, what books line her shelves, what food fills her cabinets. And, in this particular case, what size vibrator and dildo rest in plain view on the rumpled, white bed sheets.

The first time I cleaned that house was during my second or third week with Cleaning Works. I was teamed with Maria and Angela, two seasoned Clean Workers who spoke little English. Our schedule seemed routine.

They both had cleaned Deb Princeton's place several times. It was an easy job, they assured me, and the condo itself appeared hardly lived in. Maria picked the bathrooms to do; Angela, the dusting and kitchen. By default, I had the vacuuming.

As with most assignments, no one was home. I followed procedure, carrying the Hoover up three flights to work down from the top floor. The third floor was a spacious bedroom, with a full bath at the top of the stairs. All the rooms had wall-to-wall carpeting, making my job much easier. I placed the vacuum in the middle of the room, which was a mess. Clothes were strewn everywhere; packed boxes were piled haphazardly around the room's perimeter; shoes, paired and unpaired, littered the floor; a few dumbbells were tucked into the corner.

Now, Cleaning Works is a cleaning company, not a maid service, and there are peculiar rules stating what chores we are and are not expected to perform. In a nutshell, instead of straightening up a messy desk, we work around the letters and bills. Doing this drives me crazy — I mean what's the point? I figure a person is forking out good money to have someone in to clean, the least I could do is stack their paperwork neatly.

I did a quick scan of the room looking for an outlet. I spotted a cord leading from the lamp on the nightstand down behind the back of the double bed's headboard. I quickly unwound the vacuum cord and dragged it over to the bed. That's when I saw them. Smack dab in the middle of the mattress were a deluxe vibrator and the largest dildo I had ever seen. Or maybe the *only* dildo I had seen up to that point. Either way, it made quite an impression.

I turned toward the stairs. It was silly, I know, but I was embarrassed. I felt like I'd been caught in the act. *The* act. Also on the bed were several copies of lesbian porn magazines and a collection of short stories by a popular leatherdyke. Suddenly, my image of Deb Princeton, condo owner, changed. No longer did I picture her in corporate drag, briefcase in hand; now I couldn't shake the image of Deb in chaps and a leather vest.

I worked quickly then, snatching up the piles of clothes and shoes and throwing them on the bed. I vacuumed with equal speed, slamming into the legs of innocent furniture that was unlucky enough to fall into my path. I did not want to meet Ms. Princeton that day; I wanted out of her house as soon as possible.

The Princeton job was our second of five; it was quarter to four when we got back to the office. We were the last team to get in. Connie, the kind and gentle office manager, laughed hysterically when I told her about my discovery. Deb Princeton and her sex toys were the stuff of folklore around the office. She said she would have warned me if she'd known how upset I was going to get. I wasn't necessarily upset, I whined, not wanting to sound as prudish as I was feeling, but, Jeez, she *knows* we come every other week; leaving the toys out like that borders on sexual harassment! Connie, ever supportive, rolled her eyes, and continued scheduling the next day's work.

◆◆◆◆

But that was then, and this is now. And Deb Princeton is, again, a hot topic.

What surprises Kim is that no one at Cleaning Works has had a run-in — of a sexual nature — with Deb before — that is, before Hunter Stevens: self-proclaimed studette and, in my humble opinion, compulsive liar.

Hunter's the kind of person who would have you believe she's had sex with everyone with two legs and a cunt: the security guard at the museum; her hairdresser, in the backroom, between the wash and cut; the telephone repair woman making a house call. Not that such rendezvous aren't possible. Each adventure, on its own, is certainly believable. But who could believe that opportunities like these have knocked on this same woman's door over and over again? Who, pray tell, is that lucky? Hunter Stevens would have you think she is.

I won't argue.

But now Hunter is adding Deb Princeton to her list of conquests and, Clean Worker that I am, I'm curious to hear the dirt.

Kim and I have been talking outside, on the stoop of the office. There's a slight chill in the early-morning air, so everyone else is hanging out inside.

"I'll go check with Connie. Maybe you, me, and Hunter can all work together. Then Casanova can tell you the details herself."

Kim sets down her coffee and slips into the office. I try to imagine the story Hunter is going to come up with. I gulp down the rest of my breakfast, wipe my hands on my jeans, and score two in the trash can across the sidewalk with my garbage as Kim and Hunter come out.

"Morning," Hunter says, a sly smile escaping her lips.

"Talk to me, Hunter. And don't bullshit me." Months and months at this job have done away with my shyness. Vibrators on beds no longer shock me as they once did; now, I want details.

"What?" she questions, her eyebrows raised in the perfect model of innocence.

"What do you mean 'what'? Tell me about your dirty little job at the Princeton house."

"Oh, *that,*" Hunter drawls, sitting down on the step, her legs stretched out before her. "My, oh my, where do I begin?"

Although it kills me to admit it, I like Hunter. She is extremely sexy and very approachable. And though I do think she's fabricated many of her exploits, I can't deny she is popular with the girls. And for that, I am jealous.

"Well, yesterday, me, Angela, and Tara worked together. Deb's place was second on our list. We breezed through our first job — the Kelly condo on Second Ave. — and ended up at Deb's about twenty minutes early. I didn't even think about knocking or anything — I mean she's *never* home. The kitchen needed the most work, so Angela started in on that, first thing. Tara called bathrooms and started with the one on the first floor. I had vacuuming and dusting."

"Blah, blah, blah. I know how we *clean,* Hunter," I say impatiently.

"Anyway," Hunter continues, ignoring me, "it seems I should've knocked, because Deb *was* home, and she wasn't alone."

"Yee-haw!" Kim hoots. Kim and Hunter exchange high fives. Their sexual bravado embarrasses my lesbian-feminist sensibilities. Do I want to hear the rest?

"So, what happened?" I hear myself saying. So much for my personal politics.

"I'm carrying the vacuum up the stairs, and I have to stop on the second-floor landing to catch my breath. I'm either getting old or I should give up smoking. Anyway, I'm standing there and all of a sudden I hear this low moan. I think maybe I've stepped on the cat or something. Then I hear it again, so I glance into the two rooms on the second floor to see if anything is there. Nothing. So, I pick up the vacuum and start up the stairs to the top floor — Deb's bedroom. I'm about halfway up when I hear not just the moan again but a 'Yes, yes, deeper, baby, deeper.'" Hunter stops her storytelling and smiles. My eyes widen. Kim, who has already heard the story, is also smiling broadly, superior in her knowledge of what is to come.

"Needless to say," Hunter continues, "I knew it was no cat making that noise. I stop, frozen on the fourth step from the top. From the sound of things, Deb and her friend are really going at it. The bed springs are squeaking, they're breathing hard, the moaning is getting faster and faster. What's a girl to do? I leave the vacuum on the step, sneak up the rest of the stairs, and peek my head around the corner. Deb is on her hands and knees, stark naked. The other woman is wearing only that strap-on dildo we all know and love, pumping Deb from behind. I've obviously stumbled on the climax of the morning's fuck. Within seconds, Deb comes — loudly — and collapses on the bed. Her lover slowly pulls her dildo out and stretches out over Deb's back like a blanket. They both lie there awhile, basking in the afterglow. I am so hot. I'm kind of embarrassed to admit it, but I start playing with myself right then and there, praying that Deb and her friend aren't done for the day. After a few seconds, Deb opens her eyes. She stares right at me. 'Cleaning Works,' I say."

"No way," I blurt out.

"Way," Hunter counters. She pulls her knees up to her chest, wraps her arms around her legs, and rests her chin on her knees. "Do you want me to go on?"

"Of course she does," Kim answers for me.

"So there I am, hot and horny in a room with two naked dykes, one a complete stranger, the other a client. So ... I ask them if they would mind if I vacuumed around them." Hunter bursts out laughing at her own joke. I turn to Kim, roll my eyes, and wait patiently. Wiping the tears from her eyes, Hunter goes on. "The other woman — her name is Lena — nearly has a heart attack. She jumps out of bed, holding the sheet in front of her. I can't keep my eyes off Deb, though. Did you ever notice how cute she is? I've only seen her on her way out of the house; I guess I never got a good look. She's hot. And irresistible when she's naked," Hunter says wistfully.

"So, I'm standing there, staring. Finally, after what seems like a lifetime, Deb breaks the silence with 'Come here often?' I hesitate just a second before joining her on the bed, ripping my t-shirt off on the way over. Lena is still huddled in the corner, I think. I don't care. When we first start touching, it's like Deb and I each have six hands. It's amazing. She's still slick from her go-round with Lena. She reeks of sex. I'm in heaven. I take a nipple between my teeth ever so gently as I spread her thighs. A lot of foreplay seems redundant, considering, so I slip two fingers into her cunt. She moans that moan I'd heard from the stairs. She opens her thighs wider as I pump my fingers in and out; pretty soon I add two more. Jeez, it *still* amazes me to think how much room she has."

"I can't believe you're telling us this," I say. "I can't believe I'm *listening* to this."

"Oh, you love it," Kim smirks. "Keep going, Hunter."

"So I keep fucking her — though she's bucking so much it's hard to stay with her. All I'm conscious of is her cunt, her smell, and the rhythm of my hand. Then her cunt opens wider, I tuck my thumb into my palm, and she takes in all of me." Hunter pauses then, her eyes momentarily glazing over. "Damn, I love that," she says quietly. "I pump her hard. I use muscles in my arms I never knew I had. Finally, she comes. And comes. And comes. Her cunt juice is everywhere. It was amazing."

"I guess that G-spot thing is real," I say, thinking of all the experiences I've yet to have in bed.

"Damn straight. Anyway, I pull out. Deb is on her back, panting, her head hanging over the side of the bed. For that brief moment, we're in love. Then, from across the room, I hear, 'I bet you expect a tip now.' I've totally forgotten Lena is still in the room. But she is, and when I turn and look at her, and see the hunger in her eyes, my cunt starts to throb. I try to answer, but no words come. Instead, I just moan. I'm dripping wet. She saunters over to the bed, still wearing the harness and dildo from before.

"I'm still sitting in the middle of the bed. She grabs both my legs and pulls me to her, so now I'm sitting on the edge, my feet on the floor. She kneels down between my thighs. I swear to you, I have never wanted to be fucked more in my entire life. She lowers her head and blows on my cunt, softly. Then she puts her right hand, fingers spread, on top of my bush. Slowly, from back to front, she slides her thumb between my lips. I am *not* in the mood for slow and gentle, I can tell you that. I raise my hips to meet her thumb and to subtly get my point across — I don't know, 'Fuck me now' seems a bit too direct. I look down just as Lena is about to lick me. I tell you, when I see this, I can wait for the fuck. She works her tongue slowly, from my vagina up to my clit and back again. It's fabulous, so warm and wet. I start rocking to her rhythm. She starts biting me, and sucking, and licking harder. She clamps on to my clit and won't let go. It's almost too much. And just when I'm about to come, she stops. Boom. I almost die. But then, right away — I think she sees how frustrated I am — she climbs on top of me and shoves the dildo into me. She isn't gentle anymore. The dildo is slurping in and out. She's got her nails dug into my shoulders. I don't want her to stop. Suddenly, there's a mouth on mine. And it's not Lena's. Deb is back from the dead. She kisses me, hard; I try to keep up, but I don't want to lose my concentration on what's happening between my legs. It all seems too confusing; there's too much going on. Deb starts in on my breasts, taking as much as she can into her mouth. She sucks hard on my nipple. I cry out — first in pain, then, well, in pleasure. I come big-time."

"Wow" is all I can say.

"Yeah," Hunter replies. "A definite wow."

"Where were Angela and Tara through all this?" Kim asks Hunter.

"Well, after a while, Deb, Lena, and I untangle ourselves, and I realize that, technically, I'm at work. Oops. So, I get dressed, thank Deb and Lena for their hospitality, and go downstairs. Angela and Tara are watching a movie on HBO. They never said a word about it."

"Do you think they'll say anything to Connie?" I question.

"Let's hope not." Hunter smiles, her fingers crossed.

As if on cue, Connie joins us on the stoop. "Are you guys going to work today or stay out here and gossip all morning?"

"We're ready, Connie, we're ready. I'm just waiting for you to give me the keys. And where's Joyce? She's our third person." Hunter is all business now.

Hunter's teamed with Kim and Joyce. I haven't bothered to check the board to see who I'm working with. "Who am I with?" I ask Connie. I don't feel like getting up and going into the office.

"Change of plans," Connie says. "Shea Houston just called and needs someone to come this morning. She's having people in from out of town and she needs someone to help her get the place in order. It's a slow day, anyway, so I'm sending you alone."

"Why me?" I ask.

"She requested you," Connie says matter-of-factly. "You can take the blue Escort. Come get the keys." She turns and goes back into the office.

Kim and Hunter stare at me. "What?" I snap, trying hard not to let my — what? excitement, confusion? — show on my face.

"She *requested* you? Since when does Shea Houston prefer *you?*"

I think Hunter is the jealous one now.

"I have no idea, Hunter. Maybe I'm just a good cleaner, is all." I smile and go into the office to collect my supplies.

◆◆◆◆

I turn the car radio up loud. There's no use thinking too much about what Shea's requesting me means. I mean, I'm efficient. I'm always pleasant. I don't usually help myself to the contents of clients' refrigerators. Could that be all there is to it?

Shea's an interesting woman. If I didn't know better, I'd think she was definitely a lesbian. She's a good friend of Alexandra, the owner of Cleaning Works. I'm pretty sure they went to school together. Wellesley, I think, where I'm sure Shea was one of only a handful of women of color.

I've been intrigued with Shea since I first started at Cleaning Works. She's married to a guy named Snake, or Cobra, or something like that. He's a bongo player in some retro-sixties beat-poetry-performance-band thing. It's hard to explain what the band does exactly, but whatever it is, it's made them the darlings of the underground Boston scene. I've met him a few times when I've been over cleaning. He's friendly, but a little too laid-back for my tastes. I've never seen him and Shea together, though. It's always one or the other at the house.

Shea's a painter. An artist. She always wears loose-fitting 501s, splattered with paint, holes in the knees, that hang seductively on her slender hips. When she wears a sleeveless t-shirt, which is almost always, you can see the tattoo on her right biceps. It's a simple geometrical design, in black ink, that circles her upper arm and accentuates her muscles. It's amazingly sexy. I try not to stare.

She wears her hair in dreadlocks, which fall just to her shoulders. Her right ear sports about five gold hoops; her left ear, just one. Her eyes sparkle; her smile is contagious. Her skin is flawless and she wears no makeup, although her face is often smeared with paint from her day's work. If she gets bored with painting, she can easily start a second career in modeling. Simply put, Shea Houston is beautiful.

I pull up in her driveway at a quarter after nine. It takes me two trips to carry all of the supplies onto the porch. I ring the doorbell and pray that Shea answers, not her husband. Then — considering how horny Hunter has gotten me — I think maybe I'm safer with Snake.

"Hi." Shea smiles. "Thanks so much for coming this morning. The place is a wreck and my brother-in-law and his wife are flying in from Atlanta this afternoon. You're a godsend." She is wearing her standard jeans and t-shirt. She is barefoot.

I smile. "Just doing my job." She seems talkative today. Is she nervous, too? "What can I do for you this morning?"

"I have to finish up a painting in my studio before I can help you. Why don't you head upstairs and work on the bedroom and bath. Trust me, that will take awhile."

The Houston house has always seemed like a slew of contradictions to me. The house is small, very small. The side door leads into an average-size kitchen. Immediately to the left is a sun porch with a large hot tub. The living room is off to the right of the kitchen. It, too, is small, the furniture shabby, except for the black leather couch that dominates the room. Behind the kitchen is Shea and Snake's combined studio. We rarely go in there. Upstairs is a large bedroom. The floor is covered with a hideous shag carpet, worn with age. The furniture is clearly yard-sale chic. The bathroom, on the other hand, is newly redone. It has a large sunken bathtub and a beautiful ceramic tile shower. Beautiful to look at, a nightmare to clean.

I dust and vacuum their bedroom first. It doesn't take much. Because of its furnishings — battered furniture, the ugly rug — it never really can look *good,* but at least it can be clean. I really am not in the mood to start in on that bathroom, but I do, spurred on by the notion of finishing in a couple of hours and having the rest of the day to myself.

I quickly clean the toilet and the sink. They are messy, but it isn't hard work. The shower, however, is going to require some muscle. I take off my sneakers and socks (who's going to see me?) and reach over and turn on the water. The water blasts out of the showerhead. I turn it off, squirt some Soft Scrub onto the walls and floor, and climb in to tackle the scum. Once I start, I switch to automatic pilot, scrubbing and wiping with abandon. Taking care to get in between the knobs and the faucet, I accidentally turn on the water. Cold water soaks me before I can scramble to turn the showerhead off. "Shit," I exclaim. "Fuck," I add for emphasis. I finish up cleaning the shower, grab a towel from the rack, and attempt to dry myself off.

"Have a nice shower?"

I jump. "I ... um..." I can't quite get the words out.

"I do that all the time, too. Here, let me get you a fresh towel." Shea walks over to the linen closet, and I turn to glance at my reflection in the mirror. My spiky blonde hair is plastered to my head. My t-shirt clings to my breasts. My nipples are hard.

"Thanks," I say, suddenly embarrassed. When I reach for the towel, our hands touch. A spark shoots through my body. She doesn't pull away. She meets my stare. "What next?" I say to break the mood.

"Right, next," Shea says quietly. Does she sound disappointed?

We go downstairs and clean the living room and the kitchen. I get the feeling that she and her husband don't spend much time in the former: it's never messy and there doesn't seem to be much to do there. They keep the stereo in the studio and the TV in the bedroom. The kitchen is definitely used. We work for an hour straight. I'm exhausted when we finally finish. She hands me a glass of fresh lemonade.

"Man, I'm filthy," I say, as I look down at my t-shirt, which is covered with Soft Scrub and dirt. The t-shirt is damp, more from sweat by now, I imagine, than from the mishap in the shower. "Good thing I get to go home after this. They probably wouldn't let me in if I had another house to do."

"I can't imagine anyone turning you away."

What was *that?* Am I crazy, or is Shea Houston coming on to me? "Oh, you'd be surprised at some of the places we clean. At one place, we have to take off our shoes before the woman lets us in. She's afraid that we'll mess up her hardwood floors."

"I never could understand people's obsession with cleanliness. There are so many better ways to spend your time."

"Well, I'm a neat freak myself. Maybe I should get a hobby or something."

"Or something," Shea says, as she gets up and moves into the sun porch. "This is all that's left," she continues, pointing to the hot tub. "I just want to clean around the edges, and wipe down the cover. We have to be careful not to get any chemicals in the water. Do you have any energy left?"

"Sure."

"Great, let's do it."

We work together like a well-oiled machine. I scrub, she wipes. Having her next to me is pure heaven. She's so close I can feel her heat.

"It looks fabulous. I've never seen this so clean. Can you just reach over to that side and rub a sponge over that one spot?"

"You have to brace me: my balance isn't great." She grips my belt loop as I lean over and finish the job. "Done!" I say, as I sit on the edge of the tub.

"Thanks."

I realize now how tired I am, how much my body aches from working. I would kill for a chance to take a dip in the hot tub.

"I have a few hours before my guests arrive. Would you like to go in for a bit?" she asks, her eyes going from me to the tub then back to me. For a second, I wonder if Shea can read my mind.

"Are you sure?"

"Why not? Let me run upstairs and get towels while you go outside and hose yourself down." She is gone before I can reply.

I pull off my dirty t-shirt, shorts, and underwear. I thank god they don't have holes in them. Once naked, I look down at myself and am suddenly aware of just how white I am. The weather has just turned warm and I haven't had a chance to get any sun. I'm entirely too pale. I think about putting my clothes back on but instead go outside, turn the water on low, and use my hands to scrub off the dirt. The yard is surrounded by a tall wooden fence, giving me plenty of privacy. It's not warm enough to be outside naked and wet, though, so I quickly finish up and return to the sun porch. I climb slowly into the hot water and immediately feel some of the tension leave my body. Suddenly, Shea is standing in the doorway, two towels in her hand. She looks like she, too, just took a quick shower.

"Hey, this feels great. Do you and your husband use this a lot?"

"Not really. Snake and I have very different schedules. I can go days without seeing him."

I notice that Shea is staring at my breasts. I run my fingers through my hair. Can I invite her into her own hot tub? She has two towels — she's probably planning to come in anyway. "Are you going to join me? You've worked as hard as I have today."

She nods slowly. Then, she reaches down, unbuttons her jeans, and slides them over her hips. She hesitates just a moment before she pulls off her underwear, too. She puts one foot into the water.

"Don't forget your shirt, Shea." I look into her eyes. She seems scared, unsure. "I promise I won't bite."

She lifts the t-shirt over her head, revealing small, perfectly formed breasts. Breasts of a goddess. I feel a stirring between my legs. My heart skips a beat. Shy, she moves quickly into the shelter of the water.

"Why did you ask for me this morning, Shea?" Now seems like a good time for honesty. A good time for answers.

Shea sighs. "I'm not sure. Believe me — I wasn't planning anything. I mean, I've thought about you, fantasized about you even, but really I just like watching you work."

"Oh." I'm shocked. Until today, Shea has always been nonchalant. She greets the crew at the door, and then goes off to her studio. Her presence has always been strong, though. Now she's telling me that she's been watching me. Now it's my turn to feel uncomfortable. I am not sure what is supposed to happen next, but I know what I want to happen next.

"Have you ever been with a woman, Shea? Made love with one, I mean?"

"No."

"But you've wondered about it?"

"Yes."

"I'd love to be your first." I worry we sound like a bad soap opera. I smile and reach over and gently place my open hand on her cheek.

"Oh god," she says hoarsely. "I can't believe I'm going to say this." She pauses. "I want to touch you."

I move over to her so we are straddling each other, and hold her face between my hands. I kiss her, softly at first, and then harder, so she'll know just how much I want to touch her, too. "Do you know how incredibly sexy you are?" I ask her.

She answers with a kiss. And another. And another. I could drown in her kisses as easily as in this hot tub. I reach down and caress her breasts. Her nipples are dark, almost blue, and large. I suck on them carefully. She moans loudly, encouraging me. She holds my head firmly to her breast. I suck as if my life depends on it.

My left hand slides down her back, beneath the water, and cups her ass. I move away from her breast, back to her mouth. My right hand reaches behind me and runs up the length of her leg. She shaves: her skin is smooth and soft. I squeeze her thigh. We both moan. I open my eyes as I reach between her legs. Quickly and efficiently, I plunge two fingers into her cunt. Her eyes fly open, and I smile. She sucks in her breath. *"Yes"* is all she says.

I hold her to me with my left hand, pulling her as close as I can, and continue to fuck her slowly with my right hand.

I massage her clit, which is large and hard, with my thumb. I add two more fingers to her cunt. I move my left hand back around her, and gently slide a finger up and down the crack of her ass. I find her hole and massage the opening. *"Yes,"* she says again. I slowly push my middle finger into the tight opening. Shea shudders. I keep the same rhythm with both hands. Pressed to her, I feel her heartbeat. She comes quickly, suddenly. I feel her collapse against my front, spent.

She looks up at me, her eyes unfocused. "My god, what did you do to me? What can I do for you?"

"Kiss me," I say.

"Come with me upstairs," she counters.

We barely dry off before we're bounding up the stairs to her bedroom. She throws me onto the bed and flings herself on top of me. The contrast of her brown skin against mine is shocking. She holds me down by my wrists.

"I want to taste you," she says. We stare at each other for a long time.

"I won't stop you," I finally answer.

Shea slips down between my legs. I reach over my head and grab the wooden bars of the headboard. Shea is tentative at first, examines me closely. I am very wet; her fingers slide easily through my lips. She slips one finger into my cunt as she leans over and kisses my bush. I smile at her tenderness. First she replaces her finger in my vagina with her tongue. Her tongue is long and slender, perfect for the job she is doing. "Lick me," I tell her.

With strong strokes, she licks from my hole to my clit, stopping to pay extra attention to my sensitive clit. I buck. She grips my hips and holds me in place. She doesn't want to lose her rhythm. She eats me for a long time. She alternates sucking on my clit and nibbling on it. I am on the edge. She inserts a finger into my vagina. I cry out as I come.

We lie in each other's arms for a long time. For a while, Shea sleeps. I look at the clock and see that it is nearly one o'clock. Connie is going to begin to wonder where I am. Am I going to get paid for this time? The thought makes me smile. I gently nudge Shea awake. "Hey, sunshine, it's time to wake up."

She mumbles something I can't understand. All I can smell is sex. I feel a familiar wetness between my legs. Kissing her lightly, I move out of her arms, and go downstairs to collect my clothes. They are almost dry from sitting in the sun. I take a sponge and quickly clean up the puddles we left behind. Then I get my cleaning supplies together, careful not to make too much noise, and load up the car. Let her sleep a bit longer, I think.

When I'm finished, I join her again upstairs. I climb into bed and stretch out next to her. She is awake.

"Is this real?" she asks. She sounds serious, like she really doesn't know.

"Very," I say.

"Good," she responds. "I'd hate to think it's all been just a dream."

"Listen, Shea, I really need to go." I am not good at this wham-bam-thank-you-ma'am stuff, and the truth is, I don't know what to expect from Shea. Is this a one-time thing? Will we see each other again? Does she want to?

"What time is it?"

"One."

"Shit, Charles and Barbara are going to be here soon." She jumps out of bed. I think we are both relieved to be given a way out, though I still think we have to acknowledge what has happened between us.

"Um, listen. I had a great time, Shea. Thanks. I just don't want you to think I'm going to expect anything from you. Not that I wouldn't *want* to see you again, but, well, no pressure here." She smiles, but for the life of me I cannot read the expression on her face.

We hug awkwardly and kiss good-bye. She gets into the shower as I leave. "Oh, hey," she yells over the running water, "when you get back, can you tell Connie that I need to schedule another appointment?"

I whistle happily all the way down the stairs to the car.

Pale blue hydrangea

✦✦✦✦ *Jane Futcher*

I t is a Saturday afternoon in mid-November, and the air
is cold but not bitter. I am standing on a tree-lined street
in suburban Rye, New York, in front of a neo-Tudor house,
about to meet Rick's sister and brother-in-law for the first time.
It is 1972 — before AIDS, before Rick met Danny, before I had
slept with a woman and had given up the struggle to be
straight, marry, and live happily ever after. Rick has told his
sister that our relationship is serious.

On the drive from Philadelphia, Rick entertains me with
tales of gay life — the bars where queens hang out in
Philadelphia, the park where Main Line stockbrokers cruise
for teenaged boys. I am excited by the talk — it is my only
contact with the gay world — and I tell him about the straight
woman at work who turns me on when she leans over my
desk, her cleavage close to my shoulder, showing me the
correct way to glass-mount a slide transparency.

We are both nervous about spending the night with Victoria
and Hal. We are trying to be a couple, but we have never slept
together, and we are both gay — he actively, me in tortured
silence. Under those circumstances, it's hard to be comfortable.

Now here I stand, in this expensive, upper-middle-class suburb near Long Island Sound, where married people raise 2.2 children and pile sacks of gourmet groceries into their dazzling European cars. Here now are Hal and Victoria coming down the steps to greet us. Hal is dark and good-looking, wears starchy, fresh Levi's and a blue chambray shirt — the perfect weekend outfit for a Madison Avenue adman. Victoria is tall and lean, with a suntan, straight brown hair, and huge brown eyes that study me curiously. And why not? I am the first woman her 26-year-old brother has ever brought home, and she is eager to inspect the package.

We shake hands awkwardly and carry our bags into the living room. It is a living room out of *Architectural Digest* — flowered chintz slipcovers, a polished mahogany coffee table, graceful Shaker chairs. Victoria brings in a tray with tea, then crystal glasses of red wine, still later, Perrier. It is cold in the house, and I am hungry. But there is no food. Hal lights a joint. I don't smoke it. I can't afford to get more uptight than I already am.

"Where are the children?" Rick asks. He is taller than his sister and much gentler.

Not to worry, says Victoria. They are spending the night with friends and will be home for breakfast in the morning. Something is in the air. Tension, an unspoken excitement, lights his sister's eyes. Hal taps his fingers against his thigh, then runs upstairs and returns with a silver box and a small slab of marble. He has a surprise for us. Cocaine. Let's do some lines.

I have never tried cocaine. I don't know whether to be pleased or not. I ask Rick what it's like, but he doesn't know. He only smokes pots and does the occasional Quaalude. Will I have hallucinations, I whisper? Will it make me paranoid? Oh, no, says Victoria, squeezing my arm, it's subtle and electrifying. Try it, she says, showing us how to sniff the powder through a child's straw. It's fun.

I sniff the powder on the green marble slab as the bare bones of trees scrape against the windows. Hal and Rick are in the kitchen telling film-business stories. Victoria and I have moved to a loveseat in the sunroom. I notice a sour taste in the back of my throat, but I don't feel anything. We are, however, having a glorious talk, gliding toward each other in a conversational Mercedes. Victoria is next to me, her perfume drawing me closer. I have never felt so brilliant. But what are we talking about? Richard Nixon's reelection? The new shopping mall in Cherry Hill, New Jersey? I can't say exactly, but it doesn't matter. I am feeling Victoria's attention in my legs, in my chest. I am tingling all over. I realize what has happened. Victoria has awakened in me the longing that Rick is supposed to be filling. When she touches the back of my hand, I cannot find my breath.

"Are you hungry?" I am startled. Rick stands over us, studying us quizzically. He and Hal want to go out to eat. We are all vaguely hungry, but it is hard to move. If we don't go soon, Rick says, the restaurants will be closed. It is 10:30 p.m.

◆◆◆◆

The backseat of the Jaguar smells of leather and perfume. We are searching White Plains for a place to eat. Everything is closed — the Italian restaurant, the Mexican, the Chinese. Hal and Rick are in the front seat, and Hal is irritable. We consider takeout chicken from Kentucky Fried, but nobody is hungry for that. We drive back home and eat popcorn in the living room. Hal and Rick are tired. I glance at Victoria, who looks at me, then looks away. I am not tired at all, just cold and slightly numb.

I will sleep in the pink bedroom belonging to Victoria's twelve-year-old daughter, Alice. It is large and pretty, with pinups of *Vogue* models and a girl's pink dressing table and chair. Rick will sleep in little Harry's room. He and I say good night on the landing halfway up the stairs. "How are you doing?" he whispers.

"Okay, I think."

"Victoria likes you. She told me in the kitchen."

I feel giddy. My stomach whirls. "I like her, too." I glance at the Andy Warhol print of Marilyn Monroe on the wall behind Rick. "She's very warm."

"Ah." Rick rolls his eyes and raises his eyebrows uneasily. "She's crazy, you know."

Victoria looks at us from the bottom of the stairs, head cocked to one side. "You're talking about me, Rick," she says. "What are you saying, little brother?"

Rick's laugh is a little too loud. "We were saying how much we love you, Victoria."

"And I love you." His sister smiles at me and winks.

On the daughter's pink cotton sheets, I lie awake, unable to sleep. I don't realize it's the cocaine that's made me so restless. It is a strange family, I think, not eating food, only drinking beverages and sniffing cocaine. I try to guess what Rick and Hal discussed in the kitchen while I talked to Victoria. I wonder for a minute if he and Hal had sex. No. Not even Rick would get it on with his sister's husband. I take comfort in the clean smell of the sheets and the stillness of this wooden house.

The clock strikes in the hallway. It's two a.m. I hear a noise. Someone is at the door. Without switching on a light, a figure tiptoes toward me in what looks like an overcoat. "Are you awake?" It's Victoria. She sits down on the bed. The feel of her body next to mine awakens an ancient hunger.

"Listen," she says softly. "I want to take you for a ride in the Jag."

"What?"

"Don't get dressed, just put on your coat."

I stare at her dark shape. "Now?"

"Why not? You won't be able to sleep."

"I won't?"

She shakes her head. "It's the cocaine. We had more than they did."

My heart lurches. I want to go, but Victoria is on the edge, will take me to the edge if I'm not careful. But why not? What am I afraid of? Don't I *want* to go to the edge? I pull off the covers.

"Don't get dressed. Just wear your coat."

I find my blue jeans and a sweater. I am too uptight to go without clothes. The floor creaks as we descend the stairs to the kitchen. My hands sweat. I am afraid that Hal or Rick will hear us, and stop us.

Victoria is already seated in the Jaguar and indeed she is naked, save for her black sable coat. I can see her full breasts as she reaches up to click on her Magic Genie remote-control garage door opener. She drives very slowly, toward the ocean. She is talking, and as she talks she stops at an intersection in Rye. The light changes from green to red, then back to green, but Victoria does not move. "You better drive," I say, "or the cops will get us."

"Scared?" she laughs, then drops her foot onto the accelerator.

We are at the ocean now, sitting in the dark, on a jetty overlooking the water. Or maybe it is the Sound. Victoria is talking about Rick. "He's gay, you know," she says.

I nod. This is the first mention of gay, anything gay. It is a step, I know, in the direction of my craving. She is getting down to it. "I don't understand my brother," she says. "But I can understand two women being attracted to each other."

I inhale and grip the granite ledge. I feel the heat of her words. "Yes," I say. "I can too."

"Are you attracted to women?" She leans closer.

I hope the waves splashing against the jetty will drown my words. "Yes."

She says nothing. We sit in silence, the salt air chilling my cheeks, the tension screaming between us. "I am attracted to you," she whispers.

The cocaine is racing inside me. I do not feel brilliant anymore, just excited and numb. I have never been this close to a woman. I have stuffed down my feelings since first grade. I have never allowed myself an expression of my desire. And here, next to me, is my boyfriend's sister, her arm around my waist, her fingers rising beneath my sweater.

I play with the zipper of my jacket. "I've never ... not with a woman."

Her breath singes my neck. "I'm surprised."

I want to scream, right here on the jetty, in the dark, above the salt waves. I'd like to kiss her, crush her, write my name across her naked torso. "I've wanted to."

"Hal thought you had," she says. She stands up and leads me back to the car. I am blushing. I had not realized I was so obvious.

Victoria is driving slowly, weaving through the town of White Plains. Her diamond ring sparkles in the glow of the dashboard. "I find you very attractive. "

I look behind us, afraid other cars might hear us, see us, stop us. "I find you, too." The words creak out of my mouth.

She has stopped the car in the road again and has found a tape of Gladys Knight and the Pips — "Midnight Train to Georgia." She is stroking my hair.

"I'd like to go to bed with you," she says, twisting her wedding ring around her finger.

Sirens whine in my brain. My boyfriend's sister wants to go to bed with me. The electric clock ticks on the dashboard. "I would have to have a drink first," I say finally.

She laughs. "Good idea."

I have taken her hand and am kissing the tan, perfume-soaked fingers, amazed by my boldness. "I have wanted to do this," I whisper, "forever." My body is approaching meltdown. I no longer have words. She guns the car and races us back to her tree-lined street.

In the kitchen, we fumble for glasses and ice. My hands tremble as I pour out two tumblers of Chivas Regal. We stand barefoot at the counter, gulping our drinks. The scotch burns inside me, but I feel safer now, as the cold nerves of the cocaine give way to the warm fire of alcohol.

"Ready?" Her eyes are hungry, like Rick's when he talks of the men in the bars. She leads me up the back stairs to her daughter's room. She takes off her coat, drops it on the floor, lies down in the darkness. Since I was eight, twelve, fourteen, I have wanted to touch a woman. Each time I came close something happened. I shut off the ache, silenced my desire. Now here I am, about to give in, to let it run with my boyfriend's sister, who is waiting for me in the bed. She opens her arms and I slide along her long, aerobically tuned body. The feel of her woman's skin against my own softens my heart to silk. She is filling me with a certainty, a mother's pleasure, a lover's dream. Her hips move; I am feeling the heat of her. I am handling her, a cowboy coupling with his girl. She allows me, wants me to move on top of her. Marry me, she whispers. I want you to marry me. Yes, I shiver. I want you. I'll marry you.

This is like the movies, better than the movies; it is happening to me. I hear voices. Her voice, my voice. I am calling the names of all the women — the teachers, the starlets, the schoolmates' mothers I have longed for since childhood. It is dangerous and thrilling. Each moment rewrites my past and lights my future.

"What is that smell?" I ask. "Like toothpaste."

She hesitates. "Femme Unique."

"What?"

"Vaginal deodorant."

Vaginal deodorant? I'm amazed. I have never smelled vaginal deodorant before. I kiss her thighs, brush my cheek against her legs. Something bristles on my lips.

"I shave there," she whispers. She shaves her legs all the way up, between her thighs. I blink. Perhaps this is what suburban women do. They shave and put deodorant everywhere. How strange. How wonderful.

She sleeps in my arms while I lie awake, savoring this pressure of her head upon my shoulder, the heat of her breath against my cheek, the herbal smell of her hair as I inhale. She is Patricia Neal, Jean Seaburg, Greta Garbo. She is my lover, my wife. I do not want this night to end.

We are breast to breast when the morning light creeps through the curtains. Against the pink sheets, Victoria's face seems older and more solemn. She looks at me with a softness I have not seen before, and we start again, to be sure this is not a dream.

Victoria jerks up. Hal is standing in the doorway, unshaven, in a blue terry cloth robe. "You two," he says, "better get up. Alice will be home in fifteen minutes." He stares at us, wound in each other's arms, and closes the door.

I notice the African doll in a woven headdress gazing at us from her daughter's bookshelf. "Is Hal mad?"

She stretches languidly, then snuggles down into my arms. "How could he be? It was his idea."

"What?" She is so close to my face that she has three eyes.

"He wouldn't make love with me last night. He suggested I try you. Thought you might be interested."

I swallow, loosen my grip on her waist. "It wasn't your idea?"

"No." She kisses my ear.

I stare at her sable coat in a pile on the floor. "I thought you were attracted to me."

"Hey." She kisses my cheek. "Don't let go of me. We don't have time."

I hold her tight again. I search for words. "You wanted to too, didn't you, Victoria?"

The door opens again. Hal is dressed now, and angry. "Get the fuck up, Victoria. Alice is downstairs. Don't do this to me." He slams the door.

"Shit." Victoria closes her eyes, opens them, inhales, rises, and stands naked in front of me.

"I miss you already," I say. And it is true. I feel like crying.

"You're very sweet." She picks up her sable coat and leans over to kiss me. "You sure you've never done this before?"

I shake my head. "Have you?"

"First time."

"It was fun, wasn't it?"

"Very fun," she smiles.

"I'd like to do it again."

"Ah." She inhales, then closes the door behind her as she leaves.

I lie in bed, afraid to move, afraid to disturb this mesh of smell and touch and broken silence. Someone knocks on the door. Please, let it be Victoria, coming back to make love again. But it is Rick. He is pale and much taller than I remember. His brown eyes reach me uncertainly.

"Guess what?" I say slowly.

"What?" He sits next to me on the pink bed, where Victoria has been, but the feeling is so different. There is no electric shock, no molecular dissolve.

"Try to guess," I say, sitting up.

"I can't guess." He is wearing faded jeans and a red plaid shirt.

"Try."

He shakes his head. His hairline is receding. There are blue shadows under his eyes.

"Victoria and I ... were lovers." The sound of my words startles me.

His eyes widen. "What?"

I pull the covers higher, up to my neck. "We couldn't sleep, so she took me for a ride in her car, and we talked about you, and we drank scotch and then she suggested..."

"Damn her." He stands up. "Goddamn Victoria." His back is to me now as he unclenches his fists.

"What's wrong?" I have never felt so happy in my life. Rick's gay, after all. He must understand this feeling, must know what this sweet release is like.

He faces me, the color gone from his cheeks. "She did it to hurt me," he says, hovering grimly above me, hands rattling the coins in his pocket. "Me and especially Hal."

I close my eyes. Did the night have something to do with Hal and Rick? We were two women, weren't we, hungry, loving, releasing the caged things within? "It didn't have anything to do with you and Hal."

"Ah," he says, just like his sister. "You don't know her." He opens the door. He is crying.

144 ✦

◆◆◆◆

In the same alcove where Victoria and I talked for so many hours last night, we eat bagels and cream cheese with the three children — two girls and a boy — who steal shy looks at me. Hal does not speak. Rick is courteous but subdued. I glance at Victoria, who eats nothing, sips her coffee, avoids my eyes. The kids tell us about a birthday party at a bowling alley. Someone threw up and they had a wonderful time. It is strange, this change in Victoria. Is Rick right? Did she do it to hurt her husband and her brother? Once, Victoria looks at me without hiding, lets the warmth of last night show in her eyes. My legs soften, my breath races. Then her face tightens and becomes blank again.

Rick puts his dish in the sink and says it is time to drive back to Philadelphia. He and Hal load the car. Victoria offers to show me the garden. We walk arm in arm, finally alone. There is so much I want to say. But the children are watching from the window, and their eyes freeze our conversation. We go as far as we can, to the edge of the lawn, and stop to study a pale blue hydrangea that has somehow survived the November cold. We stare at the blue blossom, heartened by its triumph over the frost.

"Thank you," I say, squeezing Victoria's hand.

She glances at the house. "Rick's furious with me."

"I'm not thinking about Rick." I smile into her worried eyes. I love you, I say with my eyes. I am taking you home, holding you next to me.

Her face contorts, shocked, the way Rick's does when he talks about his parents and their hunger for him. "It seems so hopeless. Hal, the kids, Rick. All so angry at me."

Near us, a robin pecks the hard ground looking for a worm. "It was so wonderful," I say. "If they knew how wonderful we felt, they wouldn't be so mad."

She cocks her head to one side. I see the beginning of a smile. "It was fun, wasn't it?"

"Ah," I sigh, borrowing the family expression. "Very, very fun." I want to ask her to come to Philadelphia, to meet me in New York. I want to spend a whole night and a day and perhaps another night with her. I don't want to leave. But I can feel the eyes at the window, and Rick is on the back porch, calling us, telling me it is time to leave. Victoria looks at her brother, hesitates, and kisses me defiantly on the lips. Then, wordlessly, she turns and snaps off the head of the blue hydrangea.

◆◆◆◆

Rick roars out of Rye. He cannot drive home fast enough. He doesn't want to know about Victoria, about what happened last night, but I tell him anyway. I want him to understand what's happened. It's too important. My molecular structure has undergone a complete transformation. Everything looks different, even the littered on-ramps of the New Jersey Turnpike and the smog-filled skyline of Newark. I have done it. I have loved a woman. I have lost my virginity. Why did it take so long?

◆◆◆◆

For days, weeks after that November night I move in a dream. I think only of Victoria — her body, her voice, her suburban lair. She never calls, and she has asked me, without words, not to call her — because of Hal, because of Rick, because of the children. Perhaps the longing to reach her, to merge again with that lean, surprising body, is the reason I sleep with Rick soon after our trip to Rye. Her brother is kind, considerate, a gentleman in every way. And that, of course, is exactly the problem. Rick is not his sister. We will never fly together on clouds of pink. Yet the act itself seems, somehow, an odd but necessary step in the process of my coming out.

In June, I take a job in New York, and three months later, Rick moves there too. By then we are no longer lovers. By then my transformation is complete. I am in love with New York and the Duchess — a lesbian bar on Sheridan Square — and have met a Southern belle named Bettie Anne at the office where I work. Rick, still hurt and hoping he might not be gay, will not speak to me. Then one day, by the Seventy-second Street IRT, I spot him buying a newspaper at the kiosk near the entrance to the subway.

"Rick?"

He turns and smiles. We hug. We talk for a while; he tells me about the film he is making for public television. Then, with some hesitation, I ask, "How's Victoria?"

"Ah," he says, and wipes something from his eye. "She's ... had a breakdown."

"Breakdown?" I swallow. A homeless man is peeing on the sidewalk. "What happened?"

His brown eyes, the eyes of a friend now, not a lover, assess me slowly, then commit themselves to me. "She flipped out. Ran naked through the streets of Rye, not a stitch on, yelling that Hal was trying to kill her, holding her hostage in her own house. It wasn't true, of course. A neighbor called the police. They took her away in a straightjacket." Rick pauses as a noisy bus passes on Seventh Avenue. "She's better now, on the Thorazine." A Great Dane with an enormous pink tongue licks an ice cream cone from the gutter. As an afterthought, he adds, "The children are living with Hal's parents."

My heart accelerates. "I'm sorry, Rick."

He nods and bites his lip.

"Should I write to her? Call her? Is there anything I can do?"

He squints down at some broken glass near his feet. "I wouldn't," he says. "She's still..."

I feel my throat tighten.

"She has to stay calm. She can't ... A letter from you now might, you know..."

"Excite her," I whisper. And then I fade slowly down into the underground.

Anna, remembering

✦✦✦✦ *Patricia Roth Schwartz*

As the early-morning mist rises like smoke from the quilted valleys below, Anna climbs the craggy path as always, gathering basket in hand. The view, so splendid in its scope and changeability, is not something she has become used to, even in twenty years' time. Stopping to take it in like breath is a ritual, her form of prayer. She offers up as always her messages to those who have gone before her, into that realm where she senses in her marrow she herself will soon be called. Those she remembers are always the ones who shared her bed — the cats and the women, sometimes jumbled together. Now, she's alone, without even feline comfort, fearing to keep an animal that might outlive her and have to turn to the woods.

Memory, for Anna, is most of what she has left — that and the intensity of each day: the light, the scent of whatever's blooming, the play of colors across the sky, the shapes of the trees reaching up. She lives now in both the moment and the many moments of the past, laid over one another like clear sheets of cellophane, images intermingled, yet each for her distinct.

For a long time, Anna has not made love with a lover, even, to be precise, with herself, if that expressly sexual definition is applied. Her last dear companion died five years ago, having been able to remain, as she had wished, at home; Anna's daughter, as well as an intrepid public health nurse, no-nonsense in hiking boots and denims, had helped. Sylvie's ashes lay now beneath the sugar maple tree that was her favorite; when it blazes in the fall, Anna knows their passion has not died, only transformed. Having a lover now, even enjoying her own ability to coax her body into delicious explosion, seems unimportant, as the whole world, on mornings like this, is a lover, every inch of her caressed by every inch of it. She has learned, anyway, over the years as a lover of women, that there is no specific "sex act," no particular function that must take place before lovemaking becomes official.

I have been well loved and loved many well in return, she tells herself this morning as her prayer finishes and she begins to climb the trail again looking for Saint-John's-wort; mullein; wild grape, which she locates by its sharp, drunken scent; and the elusive wild blackberries, ever so much more prized than the cultivated ones along her garden fence. In her pack she carries little bottles of olive oil in which to place the buttery Saint John's flowers and the paler yellow ones of the mullein, to turn into remedies against wintertime ailments. Perhaps another winter will find her joined with her lovers gone before. Nevertheless, she gathers as she always has, to be prepared. As she picks, she begins the daily remembrances that have been her litany for weeks now, one of the reasons she believes her remaining time here will be short. Everything has been gone over and over: her childhood; her growing up; the painful family life she escaped from to nurses' school; the career — climbing the ladder to promotions, dropping out, scraping and scrimping to study naturopathy to build and gain another career, this time an alternative one — conceiving (by donor) and birthing her daughter; raising her, sometimes with the help of a lover, sometimes not. There were the many cats, the many gardens, the many women whose hands she'd held as they birthed or died or came back to full health. There was leaving the city for the mountains: first to the town, then full-time to the weekend cabin, expanded and winterized; the bitter winter months after her semiretirement spent in Florida with her marine biologist daughter; her return always in time for the almost-hidden hepatica, the trailing arbutus of early spring, followed by the wild crab apples, the wild strawberries, and the planting out of the seedlings she'd started indoors for the rows of tomatoes and peppers and eggplants.

Now, today, Anna remembers her lovers. Last week she thought of her many friends: those few still alive; the ones lost to death; the ones who did not stay the course, who took turnings that were ugly, or full of spiritual disease, from whom she had painfully to sever. Before that, many months were spent reopening, then healing, the wounds of her family. But now all that has passed somehow, been laid to rest; she allows herself instead the pure joy of remembering love and the making of love. Yes, there were those who were unfaithful, or hurtful in other ways, who, like some friends, succumbed to choices that left them unable to love or to receive it, those from whom she parted in anger or pain, those who left her the same way. But today, just now, as the tiny, delicate blossoms find their way into her gentle, nimble fingers, she chooses to remember only the loving, and, more specifically, because it is her life, her memory, and her pleasure, she thinks not to separate out each woman as an entity as she has done before, but to call up the very essence of woman as lover, each blissful aspect, savoring it thoroughly as one does the body of the lover herself.

As Anna explores the gifts the woods always have to offer her, she finds herself bringing to mind each woman she's loved, whether it was a bittersweet, brief affair, or a longer sharing of days and nights. She moves through a whole cathedral of ferns in an opening in the midst of thickly growing trees. She feels the ferns gently on her legs, lets her hands brush over them, the silky hair of women, women lovers in bed, their hair, whether long or short, loose or tousled, on the pillow. Sylvie's hair turned from burnished auburn to the most perfect of snowy whites; Corinne, years younger, nevertheless sported streaks of silver and white in hair cropped short, thick and easy to run one's fingers through; and then there was Beth, angel-Beth, the one who lied, and never left her husband after all, who lasted as long as snowflakes in April — but oh, that hair! My only long-haired lover, Anna remembers. How I loved, like the hero in an old-fashioned novel, to take out the pins, letting the tresses fall section by section on Beth's satiny shoulders. First, how she loved its perfume, its splendor on the pillow as Anna hovered above her, bringing her nipples to Beth's eager mouth. How Anna loved Beth above her, letting that silken flood stroke her bare breasts, her belly, her thighs; how she loved to twist the whole braid of it gently in her hands, as she kissed Beth fiercely with several fingers deep inside of her; how Anna's grasp would tighten as Beth's muscles squeezed Anna's fingers, as she came and came and came. Then there was Barbara, with the crisp bouncy curls; saucy Candace with the thin, baby-fine, almost colorless, brown hair that felt so soft against her cheek, just before sleeping or waking.

Anna moves on, through the woods and through her memories.

The gentle moss that clusters around the curving roots of trees reminds her always of that musky softness of hair between lovers' thighs: hair more private and secret, and something she secretly lusted over. In the early years of loving women she was not always able to express her appreciation, as some felt embarrassed, having been taught to shave and clip and hide a glorious aspect of female beauty. Sandra, whose bush was thick and springy and dark dark dark: underwear could not contain it. She seldom wore any, but when she did, to tease Anna (who loved lacy, sexy bikinis in all colors on her lovers), the hair would spring from all the edges of lace, just daring Anna to strip the panties off and plunge her tongue into that tangle of moist, fragrant wonder. And then there was Beth again, whose vulva hairs were just as silky and lovely as those of her head, who at first was shy of being admired there, of stroking and grooming and setting off the locks to make a perfect picture frame. That of Sylvie, whose hair thinned and whitened, lost the abundance it once had but still circled the greatest richness Anna ever knew. Candace had almost none, could wear the skimpiest of bathing suits and underwear with no trace. Corinne had, despite her thick, silvery head of hair, a deep black V between her thighs, almost shocking, when her pants were slipped down by an exploring hand.

Yes, Anna lets the pleasure she feels from each and every memory flow through her whole body, as she moves into a shady patch just beyond the meadow with its tall, rangy flowers, so proud in the open air and the sun, where she can nest on a rock that's part of an outcropping all along the ridge. The tiny wildflowers that like to grow in the shelter of the boulders, the blazing butter yellow of the cinquefoil, the tiny daisy of the fleabane, the plum red fragrant wild thyme in blossom, all put her in the mind of tiny things, her lovers' love buds, the clitorises they learned were there only for pleasure and delight.

First, Anna recalls discovering her own as a growing girl, the fear and the thrill of what she could make it do, how much it swelled, the strong rhythms from within, the tremendous release that followed. Then, years later, touching the first woman she ever touched other than herself, exclaiming aloud as her lover lay back, thighs spread wide in trust and anticipation, "Oh, my god, it's like touching myself!" "Yes, yes," her lover had urged, "more, more!" All the rosebuds, as privately she loves to think of them, she has licked, caressed, sucked, kissed, patted, and gently breathed upon, now seem to her to coalesce into one perfect form, swelling, ready to burst. Yet each was different: Beth's spongier, larger, temperamental, Anna finding out only later not all the orgasms she claimed really happened. But when Anna finally found that perfect combination of steady breathing, slow, steady stroking, and gentle coaxing — "It's okay, honey, okay, okay, now come to me, come to me, it's okay" — Beth's bud would grow to the size of a small robin's egg and, proudly, almost seem to burst. Candace's loved a tongue, an incessant, lapping, eager tongue; hers was tiny, hard to locate, but easy to please once found; it seemed to ask for more over and over again. The shy one was Barbara's, so shy, like wild hepatica in spring, or the even rarer Indian pipe. She'd rather have kissing and cuddling and thighs slipped between thighs for rocking, than fingers or tongue seeking out that center of all desire. Yet Anna persisted over the months they'd shared, and spent loving time coaxing Barbara's clitoris out and into its full flower. Months after Barbara left for Africa, a letter finally arrived on thin blue airmail paper, her lover writing boldly, "My rosebud misses you and what you taught her. My finger now is not the same as yours." Sylvie's, eager, quick to swell, accepting finger or tongue, was the last one besides her own Anna was to know; it seemed so familiar it could have been part of her own body. What splendid tiny flowers each of these women has shared with her.

She considers gathering these flowers now, in this shade, but knows she mustn't. Like these women, these memories, they would die if forced to exist hothouse style. Only in the wild fields of remembrances, the deep woods of love, can they survive. The little wind that whips up over the treetops seems to carry Sylvie's voice and the voices of the many others. Anna feels not so much the loss of these lovers, now, as their presence all around her, melted into the air, the sun, and the sky.

Blueberries beckon out at the meadow's other edge. Anna approaches and gathers as many as she wants, rolls the small berries over her tongue as she's rolled her tongue over the love buds and nipples of the women in her bed. She lets the sweet, tart juice coat her fingertips and lips as lovers' juices have in the past. The plump rounded curves of the berries please her as women have pleased her. She eats her fill and moves on, leaving the fruit still heavy, clustering amongst the leaves, much the way she remembers letting Barbara go when another love claimed her, the tears of pain on her pillows thick as tears of joy once were. Yet, the next summer the berries bore again and a new love ripened.

Anna feels the sun beginning to slip at last behind the tallest of the mountain peaks; she knows it's time to wind down the day's work, and begin to find her way back down the path to the cabin. But before she goes, Anna reaches down and plucks a voluptuous, rounded mushroom. Her mind focuses now on the last of her images for the day, perhaps her favorite, the breasts of her lovers: breasts that could be cradled in the palm of one hand; breasts so abundant they overflowed a two-handed grasp; young, high, taut breasts; the softer, lower breasts of older age, no less dear; breasts whose nipples were firm and distinct, having suckled children; nipples that were more girlish. There was Beth's, with that unusual inversion, one differently formed than the other, like an eye winking, which Anna had taught her to love, not to feel embarrassed by, "a special place for my tongue," she'd always said. All the colors of all the nipples — pink, reddish, brown, or pale, with almost no color — the amazing differences between them, all joyful, all appreciated, flood Anna's mind; that women can nurture and nourish each other, not just children or men, seems so delightful.

With the day's end, the remembrances of her loves come with Anna as do the herbs, berries, flowers, and roots she's gathered. All of them — Beth, Candace, Sylvie, Barbara, Corinne, others whose names she cannot now even remember, women she admired, wished to touch but never did — she remembers them all, too. Anna remembers.

The dying sun flames over the tops of the dark and steady trees as Anna, sated and content, descends toward home with her basket full, her lips and fingertips stained purple, ready for whatever the coming night might bring.

Streak of blue

✦✦✦✦   *Pam McArthur*

All the lesbians I know are marrying men and having babies. No lie. The first time it happened, I couldn't believe it. That was Maggie, a woman I'd known for twenty years. And while I'm still trying to figure out that one, I hear Marcia is having a baby.

For weeks I ponder the chance it's just lesbians whose names begin with "M." Then Jamie tells me about Rachel, who moved in with a man when she and Jamie broke up. I guess it shouldn't have been such a surprise. Rachel was only fifteen when those two got together, and she never knew any other way; it's only natural she might be curious.

And right when I think that open-minded thought, I feel the ground drop out from under me. Louise and I've been together since I was nineteen, and I never thought twice about anything else. Now with twenty years and more gone by, and all my friends' lives turning upside down, I've got to wonder about my own.

It's not a bad life, all told. Most days, I don't mind getting out of bed in the morning. And most nights, I don't mind getting into bed, either, with Louise on her side and me on mine — the electric blanket turned just right in winter, and her still under a light blanket in the dead of summer as I swelter in my plain cotton nightgown.

There's a world of detail that's Louise and me: temperatures, habits, all such a piece of me now that I can't talk about us without these little things coming out. I could easier cut off my right arm than forget what an ordinary day with Louise is like. It's like breathing, just as unconscious and essential.

And yet. And yet here I am, wondering if it wasn't all a mistake. I can't help myself; it's just the way I am. I have a question staring at me, like an ugly old moose glaring from the bushes, and I got to stare right back. And then that one question starts asking other questions, and soon I'm so bothered I don't know whether to sit down or spit.

That's what happened tonight. Maybe it was the rain that woke me, the wind hurling rain at the windows like it was going to break in, no matter what. And once I was properly awake, I started in with things like, How do I know I love Louise? How do I know I couldn't be happy with a man, when I haven't ever tried? Then I moved on to, What have I ever done with my life, I mean, anything that really matters? At least if you have children you can hope *they'll* do some good, and know that your name will be remembered for a generation or so.

I run these questions in my mind till they're all balled up in a god-awful tangle, and there's no way I'm getting back to sleep. So I lie here just trying to breathe steadily, which is not so easy when you're about to shatter your world. I feel empty inside, hollow as a chocolate Easter bunny and just as scared of being eaten alive. Eaten by wasted years, by chances not taken.

Louise shifts in her sleep, the blanket moving over my body as she turns. I widen my eyes, straining to see her in the dark, but she could just as easily be a stranger in my bed.

Rain sweeps over the house in waves. Every time I'm sure the storm is at its peak, the wind hitches up another notch. The gutters are thundering with water, the house creaking. A sudden blaze of lightning challenges the room, then leaves it darker than before. As I count the seconds till the crack of thunder, images dance at the back of my eyes. A dream catcher hanging over our bed. Shelves filled with books, some hers, some mine, all worn with time. On the top shelf, incense stands in the jar Louise made that summer she was going to be a potter. A rough, lumpy, rust-colored pot, dull as the earth it came from but for a streak of brilliant blue shot through the glaze. Louise wanted to throw it out, but I kept it. It was the truest thing she ever made. The most like her.

The dull boom of thunder comes as I slowly count to ten, and I say to myself, Two miles. Louise stirs again, slanting herself alongside me. I think about how, over the years, it's gotten easier and easier to see only the dull, lumpy clay of her and miss the blue streak. While I struggled to be a writer, following a fanciful muse, Louise was a rancher, never wanting anything else. She moves over the land like it's a part of her, like she couldn't breathe without it, and like it's enough. That's something I never understood, even though I see it with my own eyes.

Fact is, twenty years ago, when my friend Jane told me about this woman I had to meet, I couldn't have been more astonished.

"*New Mexico?* What on earth would I do in New Mexico?"

Jane flashed a wicked grin. "You see this woman, I lay ten to one you'll think of something."

"I've never left New England, or wanted to. It'll never work."

"Just give it a chance. There's something about her."

I didn't believe it, not for a second. But Jane badgered and bullied and it wasn't like her to play matchmaker, and I was tired of typing receipts at my father's shipping company. So I finally took a plane westward from Connecticut. The land got wider open and flatter and, finally, drier than week-old porridge. Pillars of rock and sawed-off cliffs looked both strong and precarious. It was inspiring, and I thought I would write about it when I got back home. But I never once thought a person could give her life to that land.

I don't know what Louise was expecting when I got off the plane in Albuquerque, don't know what Jane had said to arrange my stay at her ranch. But from the moment I saw her, I was worried. I'd known a few women before, but it was all in fun, nothing I had to take seriously. And I knew with one look at Louise that if we ever got anywhere, it was going to be serious down to the bone.

It wasn't because of her looks, though lord knows she was attractive in a lean and rugged sort of way. Tall and wind-blown, and very much at home in her dusty blue jeans and leather boots. Dark hair, carelessly cut, crowning her with ragged curls. Her nose was aquiline, her mouth too large to be beautiful but just right for the way she grinned at me. Crow's-feet already, dancing around warm hazel eyes, though she wasn't much older than me. When she bent to pick up my bags and throw them lightly into her pickup, I caught a flash of soft white skin just below the darkly tanned V of her neck. The suggestion of a curve there left me breathless.

All in all, I could've fallen for her on looks alone, but that wasn't what had me worried. There was something else about her, a glimpse of rock-hard determination, that told me she would not be trifled with. But I sure did want something from her, and I figured a time of reckoning would come, sooner or later.

We started out casually enough. Louise took some time off and we toured around. Taos, which I love, bursting with artists and artisans. Bandelier, a honeycomb of caves set into cliffs high above a river; we climbed steep tree-trunk ladders, worn smooth by thousands of hands and feet, to sit in the ceremonial cave that looked out across a far-flung valley. She took me to Acoma, and into silent mission churches, and through the black lava beds of the badlands, just as bleak as I had imagined.

Finally, like there was nothing else left to do, she took me home, put me on a horse, and showed me her land. We rode under formations of striated red rock, across hillsides of shale dotted with saltbush and yucca, twisted juniper and piñon pine. She reined in her horse when we reached the grassland where the river ran, hemmed in with cottonwood, tamarisk, and willow.

"Beautiful, isn't it?" she cried as she flung her hand across the windblown grass.

"Beautiful," I dutifully replied, my hand clutching the saddle horn. Walk, jog, lope, it was all the same; with each stride, her beautiful land crashed into my tailbone.

"Go with the horse; *feel* the gait," she encouraged me.

"That's the problem. I feel it too much!" I felt it in my backside all that day and could hardly walk the next. That evening she took pity on me and rubbed me down with horse liniment. I felt shy stripping down in front of her, but her hands were firm and businesslike, as if I were no different than one of her horses or stocky shorthorn cattle. Just at the end, her hands seemed to linger lightly over my skin, and it set my pulse racing; but when I looked at her, breath held, she turned away.

That was the first, tentative move. There were many more, sometimes withdrawn before the other could respond. I don't know what-all Louise was thinking, but I know I was terrified. I wasn't sure I was ready to promise forever to a woman, but that did seem to be where we were headed.

Louise was the one who settled it, finally. She asked if I would live with her. Dodging the real questions, I said, "But what will the neighbors say?"

"Let 'em talk," she said stubbornly, and went out to ride fence in the east pasture.

Talk they probably did, because I stayed. And if they knew the things we did, in Louise's four-poster bed and in the blue gamma grass of her pastures, they would've had plenty to talk about. But we worked hard, and her cattle brought good prices at the ranchers' auctions, and her team of Belgians held their own in pulling contests. Over time, the families around us gave us honest, ungrudging acceptance. Scarcely knowing what we were doing, we found we had built ourselves a comfortable life.

But comfort isn't the standard against which I want my life to be measured, and tonight I can't shake the fear that I've made the wrong choices. After flouncing in bed and punching my pillow a bit, I give up trying to sleep and go to stand by the window. The rain is still slanting fiercely against the house. I know it must be running over the baked earth, into the irrigation ditches that feed our wheat fields.

"Wheat," Louise once told me, "is not native to this land, but it's a good cash crop." To feel closer to the land, she also grows crops that have been planted in that soil for hundreds of years: squash, beans, and maize.

"What's maize?" I had asked.

Now I know her crops almost as well as she does, and tonight I watch the rain, welcoming it to our land. I smile, realizing that I am thinking like a rancher, like Louise. Another flash of lightning crackles nearby, and I count automatically.

"Under a mile," says a drowsy voice from the bed, when thunder shakes the house.

Startled, I turn toward the sound. The darkness is total and I cannot see Louise, but after a moment her voice continues.

"There's a thunderstorm every two seconds somewhere on this earth, but it's always a miracle to me."

She comes out with these tidbits at the most unlikely times; that's a part of her that delights me. And the sound of her voice reassures me, rooting me in our daily life together. Figuring maybe I can stand to talk about my uncertainties, I ask slowly, "Do you ever have any regrets? About your life, I mean."

"Sorry I didn't buy that bull at auction last year." She chuckles, and the sound is self-assured, not at all regretful.

"I was thinking more about purpose-of-life kind of stuff." I take a breath. "Are you ever sorry you didn't have kids?"

There is a long pause in the darkness. When Louise answers, her voice is fully awake. "With you, perhaps yes, I would've liked to have had a child. But it wasn't an option twenty years ago, and it's a bit late for us now, isn't it?"

I smile ruefully. A bit late; a lost chance. I ask, "Don't you ever feel like something's missing? Like you're not making any mark on the world?"

Again, a pause in the darkness. Then Louise says, "What we do have — you giving yourself to your writing, I to the land — that's our promise to the future. It's enough."

I realize I've been holding my breath, waiting for her answer, and I let the air out all at once. There is a rustling from the bed, then a raspy sound, and a tiny flame leaps up, emitting a scent of sulfur. Louise touches the burning match to a candle and the room comes to wavering, shadowy life.

Once, I thought it was romantic that she kept candles by the bed.

"Electricity goes out all the time," she said. "Pain in the ass." And I sulked for weeks, another illusion shattered. Then I realized that no matter why she stocked the candles, she also used them for pleasure. Romance and pragmatism living side by side, each as strong as the other.

In the candlelight, she holds her hand out to me. I move to the bed.

"Do you remember the first time we made love?" she whispers, and a thrill shoots through me. "I was so — awestruck — dumbfounded by the power you gave me, I was almost afraid to use it."

I lie down next to her. "I couldn't believe I was actually touching you," I remember. "I had wanted to for so long."

"We were so gentle," she continues. Her voice is soft, and it holds me halfway between sleep and desire. Then she turns to me. "I don't want to be gentle tonight."

I groan as if she had touched me, and suddenly I want her desperately. Rising up over her, I pull her to me and kiss her, the familiar face of my beloved, the eyes, the hollow of her throat, the sinewy shoulder. I am dimly aware of the roar of rain as she throws her arms around me. We wrestle in a tangle of bedsheets. My leg is planted firmly between her thighs and she rocks hard against me as we grapple like teenagers. Her hands reach for my breasts; my breasts strain for her touch. There is a bright aching, nearly intolerable, at the center of my being, and heat radiates outward from that center, singing along every trembling fiber of my body.

Nightgowns are hurled from the bed and we grab fistfuls of each other; her lean and hardened body, my stockier, rounded flesh. Candlelight plays over our bodies, light and shadow making us mysterious. I reach for her with fierce passion. Kissing downward from her shoulder, I pull her breast into my mouth. I hold her absolutely still for one exquisite moment, all movement stopped, breath held in expectation; then my tongue laps hard over her nipple. Over her hard nipple. Over and over.

"Yes, oh yes, oh yes," she cries. "Just like that, just like that, just like that."

Her feet drum the bed, beating the rhythm of a runaway horse. She is gasping against my neck, and my hand strokes roughly down to her thighs, rubbing the thick, curly hair that is arching to meet me. Galloping into my hand, she twists on the bed, lunging away from me, then back. A wild horse running the arroyo, plunging uphill, the muscles of her hindquarters tight and slick with sweat.

I press firmly through wet, heated flesh. Her musky scent fills the air, driving me wild. As she moves under me, I slide my hand down, fingers spreading desire till I tap at the dark, tight hole of her ass. She clutches me and short, sharp cries sound at my ear as she rides my hand.

Power mounts in me as I call her passion and match it with my own, biting her neck and shoulder as she writhes under me. The wild mare finds her mate, and trembles, spreading her legs boldly and screaming her lust.

"Oh — oh — oh—" Her voice climbs, a spiral of desire, until she is desperate in her hunger. "Take me, take me—"

And I do. I buck into her, plunging inside as I muffle my own cries against her breast. One hand deep in her, the other spreads her even wider open and settles at last on her rising clitoris. She is climbing me now, wild, and I rub hard and fast as she wails a high note of pure, unself-conscious passion. Her voice catches and she thrusts against me, holding hard, climbing higher and higher until she flings herself wide open on the bed. I fall on her, but she rolls me over and rides me from above. Filled with urgency, she shouts as she mounts the final crest and flies free, free, free...

Collapsing softly onto me, she holds me for a long moment. I am half-asleep, listening to my heart gradually slowing its galloping beat, listening to the thunder moving away across the plains, when she kisses me and says, "Thank you."

I look at her, breathing there against me as she has these past twenty years. Then I lean over to blow out the candle, and settle back into the pillows. I am happier than I have been in weeks. I know one midnight conversation, one hour of passion, won't answer my questions. But it helps, it helps. It sweetens the search.

In the morning I awake early to find Louise still curled against me, the sky filled with shimmering blue.

Telefon

✦✦✦✦   *Susan Wade*

It is quarter after five. I still have time.

You will call me in fifteen minutes to let me know you are at Fantasia's. We are meeting there to see Paula Winston's new film, *The Bride's Bride*.

This is your first time in the theater, so I have instructed you to go to the antique telephone booth in the balcony and call me when you arrive. It is one of those old-fashioned telephone booths that in the thirties and forties one would find in diners and train stations. Its frame is all wood and thick panes of glass extend from top to bottom. It still has the original adjustable wooden stool. The frosted globe on the ceiling once shone brightly over long-forgotten callers. But, I know the light doesn't work anymore.

I quiver with anticipation as I turn the car's ignition key. The powerful engine roars to life and I feel the vibration of the idling engine through the floorboard, accentuating the vibrations coursing through my body as I play over in my mind the little game I have planned for our evening. I have in store a very special greeting for you! Already I can feel a familiar, welcome, warm tingling between my thighs.

Pulling onto I-85, I glance at my watch. It is 5:19. Still plenty of time.

I swear vehemently as I'm forced to ease up on the accelerator. There is an accident ahead and cars are beginning to back up. Thank goddess the traffic isn't as heavy as it will be in another ten minutes.

Coasting along behind the gray Lexus in front of me, my right foot hovering over the brake, I am reminded by the glowing digital clock on the dashboard that I only have eight minutes to make my way to the theater. I take my left hand from the wheel and allow my fingers to tiptoe under the hem of my skirt and over the tender inside of my right thigh. Lightly, I begin stroking the flesh beneath my stockings. The feel of my own fingertips on my skin reminds me of your hands on me. I shudder with the remembrances of the passions we've shared.

Finally, I am past the accident scene. I wait until I am clear of the police cruiser and floor the accelerator. My nipples are rocks of tingling flesh against the lace of my bra. The Monroe exit surprises me and I must whip the wheel hard to the right to make the ramp. My recalcitrant fingers were boldly tickling my swollen clit, and I had been distracted. The driver behind me blares his horn in angry surprise as I cut him off.

I remove my hand from beneath my skirt, smooth the bunched material over my knees, and lick my fingers.

It is now 5:26. Four minutes. I am less than two miles from Fantasia's Theater.

Checking my appearance in the rearview mirror, I smooth a strand of hair as I turn into the parking lot behind the theater. I see your Nissan parked beside the building. I squeeze my car in next to yours.

I lock the car door, drop the keys in my jacket pocket, and turn toward the theater. I scan the sidewalk beside the building, making sure you are nowhere in sight.

My watch reads 5:28. Perfect!

As I walk quickly along the sidewalk, I can feel the wetness of my cunt. The juice forms a slick lubricant as my lower lips rub together with my strides. It is a lovely sensation.

Five-twenty-nine. I scan the lobby as I pay my admission. The ticket-taker tells me the movie began at 5:15. I grin and purr, "It's just part of the plan." Her brow crinkles in confusion. I just smile again and walk into the lobby. I catch a glimpse of the hem of your skirt, your calves, ankles, shoes, as you ascend the stairs to the balcony. My smile broadens. I cross the small lobby in four long strides and begin up the stairs, forcing myself to take my time. I want to make sure you are in place.

As I reach the balcony, I turn toward the telephone booth. You are there, the receiver cradled between cheek and shoulder, facing away from me. Good. And you've left the booth door open. Very good!

My steps are light, so you do not notice my approach. You have just finished dialing as I reach the corner of the booth. You straighten and hold the receiver with your left hand. The fingers of your right hand slowly, sensuously, stroke the dark, finely grained wood, worn smooth and shiny with use and time. I wait, holding my breath, until I hear you speak into the phone.

Delight tingles along my spine to my vagina as I hear you ask to speak to me, my name purring from your lips. I move quickly into the booth behind you, closing the door as I do. Startled, you try to turn, but I push my body against your back, preventing you from moving. You begin to struggle. You do not realize who I am. I quell your thrashing by moving my open mouth to the hairline along your nape, nipping at the sensitive skin. A small cry escapes your lips;

you recognize me by my mouth on the back of your neck! I know you are smiling. I can feel muscles contract and relax beneath my lips.

The door into the theater swings open and a young woman in denim shorts and a t-shirt walks by us, her head snapping in a double take as she passes us. I glance at her through the booth glass and wait until her discomfort urges her to move on to the restroom. Your eyes closed, you are oblivious to her intrusion.

The woman hurries on to the ladies' room, twice looking over her shoulder. My hands begin moving over your hips and thighs, as my mound grinds into your ass. I can feel the electric heat of you through the material of my skirt. I am rotating my hips against you, the pressure teasing my clitoral ridge. You are pushing back into me, your hips moving in rhythm with mine. Your lips part and a moan escapes. I can hear my secretary in the receiver asking you if you are there. I take the instrument from your hand and whisper "No" and depress the receiver button. The cord from the receiver to the phone is only two feet long, but I move the receiver along your body, pushing you closer as I run out of cord.

I see your nipples harden under your blouse as the mouthpiece rubs over your breasts. My breath catches as the intensity of my desire to suck them engulfs me. But, I have a plan, and my own lust must not deter me from achieving my goal of your gratification. I move the receiver slowly, circularly, around the party-hats your hard nipples have become. The distance between the mouthpiece and receiver almost perfectly captures both knobs at once.

My mouth is roaming unchallenged along your nape, around to the sides of your throat. My breath is hot and moist and my tongue is taut on the silky skin of your neck. You begin to writhe, baring the milky skin of your neck to my hunger.

Our breathing quickens; the glass of the telephone booth fogs.

My other hand has forced itself down your belly on its journey toward your bush. Even at this distance I can feel your wet heat rising through your skirt. I stroke your inner thighs through the fabric. Your hands have moved back to my hips and you are controlling — with gentle, guiding pressure — the rhythm of our dance.

I sense an intruder outside of the booth. The young woman has returned and she's standing, slack-jawed, just behind the booth, watching us. I grin at her, but do not move from you. Let her watch as this woman pleasures her lover! The thought of an audience exhilarates me, and I intensify my fondling of your breasts with the receiver. I am electrified by the quickening tempo of your hips bucking against me. My pleasure escapes my lips in a little whimper.

Bunching your skirt up around your waist, my hand finds its way up your inner thigh. I tremble with excitement as my hand touches your garter belt and stockings. I let my fingers lightly brush against the hard, pulsing button of flesh that I know so well. You exhale hoarsely at that casual touch, but I do not linger; my fingers continue their journey down the other inner thigh, and back again. Each time I move close to that intoxicating heat, I pause, letting my fingertips graze your throbbing clit. With each stroke, I increase the pressure. Your breath is raspy now. Dropping the receiver, my free hand roughly spreads your thighs and forces one leg up until your foot is resting on the stool.

You are open. Your pussy is mine! Your panties are soaked and my fingers are soapy with your pungent foam. I slip two fingers inside the waist of your panties and pull them down. Pausing, I tug gently at your wiry hairs. And finally, my fingers are poised at your pulsating orifice. I begin by teasing the rim with slow, deliberate circles.

You are groaning without pause now, your breath steaming the glass. I allow my probing digits to move slightly into the cave of your pussy. With a gasp, you turn your head to nibble at the tender flesh of my neck. I love to feel your lips on me. Moving to my ear, you whisper hoarsely: "Fuck me. Please fuck me, baby!"

I turn my head and capture your begging lips with my own as I ram two fingers deep into your hole. Your hot cunt sucks at my fingers. A low moan forms deep in my throat. I am so excited fucking you!

You are wild now, bucking against me like a dime store ride gone amok. I cry out in ecstasy and plunge a third finger deep into your gushing cunt. My hand is pumping you, deep, hard. Suddenly I withdraw, stopping the fever-pitch. I begin again, slowly and designedly. Casually I slip my fingers into you, then back out again; my strokes remain slow and purposeful. Your tunnel greedily nurses on my three fingers. You are whimpering, begging me to fuck you, to fuck your pussy hard, but I refuse. You try to increase the tempo of your hips' motions, but I firmly hold you still. You whine "Please!" Teasing you, I pull out and wait. You turn to me, your lips covering my cheeks, my neck, my mouth. "Please! Please, baby! I want to come! Please, oh please fuck me!"

I consider your request a moment. Your pleading eyes crumble my reserve and I kiss you hard and once again plunge my fingers deep inside you. You moan loudly as we kiss.

I begin to fuck you. I know now you will come soon. I must make you come hard! Gradually I increase the pace of my thrusts, each reaching deeper and deeper into your vagina. I can feel the ridges of the walls of your cunt. Your pussy is pulsating like a separate, living entity, and each contraction pulls my vulpine fingers deeper inside of you.

We are moving in a fiery rhythm. You begin to whimper. I know you are close to climax. Your cream is so hot my fingers feel as if they are melting into you. I lean my mouth into your ear and whisper my demand: "Come to me baby. I want you to come to me!" You begin your solo crescendo to orgasm. I am fucking you furiously, croaking over and over: "Yes! Yes! Oh! Yes, baby!"

Bracing your hands against the wall of the telephone booth, you push back against me hard, tensing, and silence a scream. My palm fills with your hot nectar. I slow the thrusts and bury my fingers deep within you, enjoying the sensations of your vagina's satisfied contractions. You lean back into me, panting against my throat. I can feel our hearts pounding in unison. As our breathing and pulses slow, I gently withdraw my fingers from your now quieting tunnel and let your skirt fall, wrinkled, into place. I raise my hand to my mouth and lick your sweet juice from my palm. Then, at your smiling request, I offer my fingers to you and you suck your juices from them.

Opening the door of the booth, we step out into the balcony lobby and take deep breaths, smiling at one another. My arm circles your waist and you lean into me. We kiss, sweetly, tenderly. I move my lips from your mouth, along your cheek to your ear, and whisper my love. You smile and answer with a kiss on my earlobe. We turn to enter the auditorium and I am surprised to see the young woman still standing there, shifting from leg to leg, her denim-covered thighs whispering against each other.

I smile broadly at her; you look at me puzzled. Then, tilting my head, I hold up those same three fingers and smile apologetically: "Sorry, all gone!"

A working dyke's dream

♦♦♦♦ *Karen X. Tulchinsky*

When I first started working at Gulliver's Travel, my
boss was a balding, middle-aged man named Sey-
mour Plotkin. Two months ago, he had a nervous breakdown
after his wife ran off with their gardener. For a week I didn't
have a boss. The following Monday I was sitting at my
computer when the front door opened. I heard footsteps
approaching and looked up to find a beautiful woman standing right in front of my desk. She was smiling right at me. I
smiled back as she stuck out her hand.

"Hi," she said, "I'm Sadie Singer, the new manager."

I knew I was supposed to stand up, shake her hand,
introduce myself, show her around, all that normal stuff, but
I couldn't take my eyes off her soft full lips, her finely
sculpted cheekbones, or her big brown eyes that melted right
through my Monday morning haze. With gargantuan effort, I
raised my hand and took hers, desperately forcing myself to
give her a businesslike handshake, when really I felt like
raising her hand to my lips and planting a tender kiss on her
smooth olive skin. My knees were shaking as I pushed my
steno chair backward and stood up. I was just a little taller

than she was. My eyes met hers. She was a goddess. A short, voluptuous, brown-eyed, frizzy-haired movie star. She had walked right off the pages of *People* magazine and into Gulliver's Travel. She was too glamorous to be in the travel business. I must be on "Candid Camera." I looked around for Dom Deluise.

"You must be Alexandra...," she said in a deep, husky ex-smoker's voice.

"Please," I begged, "call me Alex. Everyone does."

She held onto my hand a beat longer than necessary.

"All right ... Alex." She smiled and dropped my hand. It plunged back down to earth and hung limply at my side, my fingers vibrating from her touch. I stared into her eyes, silently thanking whatever higher power had caused Mr. Plotkin's wife to run off with a younger man so that I could be blessed with a boss like Sadie Singer. A working dyke's dream. A boss who looks like Bette Midler, Madonna, Jessica Lange, and Queen Latifah all rolled into one. Instead of answering "Yes, sir" to a fat, middle-aged man, I would now be working with a Hollywood bombshell.

"Alex, why don't you show me around. Then I'd like to start in on organizing my office. I understand Mr. Plotkin left in a hurry and that things are in some disarray."

Please, allow me to show you the inside of the supply cupboard, or better yet, my apartment, I wanted to say. "There's not much to show," I said instead. "We're pretty small. Just me, Jack — he's off sick today — and Jerry over there." I pointed to my co-worker, a flamboyant old drag queen who dressed as butch as he could during the day so he could make a living in the business world. Even then, he looked like Diana Ross in a three-piece suit, or like an older Michael Jackson before his last two nose jobs. Butch and femme both at the same time.

I led the way to the back of the storefront office so I could introduce Sadie to Jerry. She followed behind me so closely I could almost feel her nipples pressing against my back. It was growing warmer inside the office and I reached up and undid the top button of my shirt.

As we approached, Jerry stood, stuck out his hand, and half curtsied. "Well, at least you're a better dresser than poor old Mr. Plotkin. No wonder his wife left him."

"Thank you, Jerry," Sadie laughed. "I'll take that as a compliment."

I led my new boss over to the lunchroom, which had a small fridge, a coffee machine, and a table and chairs. At the very back was an oversize closet that we called the supply room. Inside, I began pointing out the elaborate inventory system that Mr. Plotkin had set up. There were stacks of vacation brochures, corporate flight planners, and travel-insurance folders to show her. I had my back to Sadie as I opened drawers and cupboards to let her see inside. When I turned around I saw that her eyes were all over my body. For a moment I didn't know if she was straight or gay. I could feel a fine sweat forming on my skin, and I casually rolled my shirt sleeves up to my elbows. I spent a long time explaining where we ordered the Xerox paper, while in my mind I could see myself leaning her up against the shelves and opening her buttons slowly, one by one, until her magnificent breasts leaped out at me. Silently, she would guide my hand underneath her skirt and I would feel her wetness calling me up inside of her, and there, in the closet, I would plunge my fingers into her, and she would urge me on and on, until she was coming and calling out my name. Her back would be indented by the stacks of Club Med brochures, but she wouldn't care. She'd lean back after and have a cigarette and maybe give me a raise and invite me home to dinner.

"Fine." Her voice came out of nowhere, bringing me back from my fantasy. "I think we've covered the supply room quite sufficiently."

"Right," I agreed, wiping the sweat from my forehead with the back of my hand.

Somehow I made it back to my desk without laying a hand on her. She went into her glass-enclosed office and began going through the files. From where I sat I had a clear view of her. Whenever she'd reach for a manila folder on her desk, she had to bend slightly, teasing me with the sight of her ample cleavage. Every so often she'd glance in my direction and I was sure she was checking me out, too. I pretended to enter words into my keyboard. I shuffled papers from one side of my desk to the other, but all the while I had one eye on Sadie and the other turned inward to watch the scores of fantasies being projected inside my head. All that morning, I was a one-woman porno production company. If I could have captured the images on film I'd have made a fortune in the X-rated-movie business. By lunchtime, in my dreams, I had seduced my sexy boss in every inch of the office, and had kissed and fondled and fucked her on every available desk, photocopier, and fax machine.

At noon, I still had one eye on Sadie as she casually freshened her lipstick. With all the care she was taking with her appearance, I knew she must be meeting someone. I pretended to be concentrating deeply on the Air Canada flight information on my monitor as she walked past me, saying she'd be back at one o' clock.

"You bet," I grinned. "See you then." I watched her walk by my desk. She couldn't see me now, so I took the opportunity to devour her from behind. She was so femme I almost died at the sight of her. I could have sworn she was wearing those old-fashioned stockings with the seams up the back.

Her perfume wafted into my nose and I swooned, breathing deeply her womanly scent. Her ass was perfect, just how derrieres were meant to be — round, full, and big, bouncing and dancing from side to side as she sauntered out the glass front door and into the street. I felt like a teenage boy in the fifties who had just gotten his first glimpse of Marilyn Monroe. My heart was racing, my palms sweating, my eyes singing a hundred rhapsodies to her. The second she was gone, I switched off my screen, grabbed my jacket, and yelled back to Jerry. "See you at one. Out for lunch."

"Better watch out, girlfriend," I heard him call out as I dashed for the door. "Business and pleasure are like oil and water. Take it from me."

There are times in a dyke's life when she just has to be crazy. There's no accounting for it. It happens out of the blue, on days that start out like any other day. I knew that right now I was just this side of doing something reckless, but I couldn't stop myself.

Before I knew exactly what I was doing, I was out in the street. Ahead of me I could see Sadie. It took another few blocks before I realized I was following her. I stayed close to the wall so that, in case she turned around, I could duck into the nearest shop. I didn't want her to see me, but I knew I wanted to see who she was meeting. Woman or man? Husband? Lover? Friend? I needed to know if she was straight or gay or what. I didn't stop to think about how ridiculous I was being. There was no time for that. I didn't want to lose her.

At the sky-train station, she took the escalator down to the mall under the big office towers. It was one of those fast-food fairs, with pizza and Chinese food and falafel stands all around the perimeter and hundreds of orange tables with yellow plastic chairs attached to them in the middle. Between noon and one on a weekday, the place is packed. Perfect. I could find a seat far enough away to be hidden, yet close enough to see what Sadie was up to. Keeping a respectable distance, I followed her down into the mall. For a moment I almost lost her, so I hurried forward, pushing people out of my way to get ahead.

At the bottom of the escalator two businessmen blocked my way. I shoved one a little too hard.

"Hey!" he shouted. People all around us turned and stared, including Sadie, who stood a few feet away against a wall. Standing beside her was a tall, thin, suit-wearing, short-haired woman who was a dyke for sure and a butch to boot. I gawked, feeling the blood rise in my cheeks. Sadie's eyes were locked on mine. Foolishly, I gripped the escalator handrail for support. It rolled around on its track and pulled me down with it. My eyes were jerked away from hers by the force, and I heard Sadie start to giggle. By the time I struggled back to my feet, all I could see was her beautiful back as she and her butch disappeared into the lunch-crowd abyss. I clapped my hands together in joy. Yay! She's a dyke. There's hope after all.

Now, I know some women would have taken the appearance of Sadie's girlfriend as a red light. She's taken, stay away, stop lusting after her. As for me, I took it as a sign of encouragement. A challenge, yet not an impossibility. If she had been meeting a man for lunch, I might have backed off. I've chased enough straight women to know what a waste of time that can be. But Sadie was clearly a femme lesbian, my favorite species, my raison d'être, the object of my tremendous desire. I smiled all the way back to the office.

When Sadie came back from lunch I did not look up. I was furiously poring over flight schedules on my computer. I could smell her perfume and knew she was standing right in front of my desk.

"You shouldn't spy on people," she said. "It's not nice. Besides, it's dangerous. You might find out something you're not supposed to know." I looked up with one eye closed, as if I was scared she would hit me or something. I saw that she was half smirking as she turned on her heels and swished toward her glass-enclosed, semiprivate office. I guess I should have been embarrassed. Strangely, I was not. I felt light, even happy. Now I had something to look forward to. Someone to chase. Work can be so boring when you do it every day. But now I had a boss I could fantasize about. Some people live their whole lives and never have such a looker for a boss. Others have that kind of luck all the time. I was happy to have it just once.

Later that afternoon I felt bold. I got up and knocked on her office door. She was standing by the filing cabinet. The top drawer was open. She looked up at me, her eyes smiling.

"Yes, Alex? What can I do for you?"

Looking her straight in the eye, I said, "If you ever need me for ... anything..." I hesitated for a moment to drag out my meaning. "...here's my number at home." I handed her one of my business cards with my private number scribbled on the back. Without taking her eyes off me, she reached for the card, her fingers grazing mine.

"I'll put it in a safe place," she said teasingly and I almost died, because she took the card and slipped it down her shirt between her breasts. I wanted to be that card. I smiled and sparkled my eyes at her. She laughed, touched my face lightly with her hand, turned, and went back to work.

On Friday night I went out to my favorite dyke bar with my best friend, Fay. We were standing near the dance floor having a beer when I saw, across the room, sitting at one of the cozy, intimate tables near the wall, Sadie and her girlfriend. I watched them for a while, and when the girlfriend got up to go to the women's room, Sadie walked over to where I was standing.

"What are you doing?" she whispered into my ear, so that I could feel her hot breath on my skin.

"What?" I turned and looked at her.

"You've been watching me all night," she challenged.

I looked down at my shoes. "Well, yes, I have, but I really can't help it." I looked up at her and she was smiling, like she was flattered, so I continued. "You really are beautiful. You're the best-looking, sexiest boss I've ever worked for."

She reached over, took my hand, and squeezed it. I stared deeply into her eyes. "I just want you to know one thing," I said recklessly. "I'm going to keep on cruising you until you either say yes ... or stop." She raised her eyebrows at me like she was amused and impressed at the same time. Then she let go of my hand and walked away.

On Monday Sadie was later than usual getting into work. At ten o'clock the front door swung open and she stomped past my desk, marched into her office, and slammed the door. All morning long, she paced, she opened drawers and banged them shut, crumpled pieces of paper into tight little balls and threw them into the garbage can across the room. For part of the morning, she sat at her desk quietly staring into space. I decided she must have had a fight with her lover. Her mood had all the markings of marital hell. I figured it was best to just stay out of her way.

At five o'clock, Jerry and Jack said good-bye for the day, but I was behind in my paperwork, so I decided to work late to catch up. I was deeply engrossed in my computer screen when I smelled Sadie's perfume drifting toward me. I looked up when she was standing right over me.

"Yes," she said, her deep brown eyes penetrating mine.

"Yes?" I was in shock.

"Yes."

I shut off my screen. "Now?"

"Now."

"Here?"

She looked around, grabbed my hand, and dragged me toward the lunch area. "Here," she said as she pulled me inside the supply room and locked the door.

As much as I had been waiting, dreaming, hoping, and praying for this moment, I needed to know why. I stepped back. "What's going on?" I asked her.

She sighed deeply and leaned against stacks of "Experience Alaska" pamphlets. "The bitch has been cheating on me. I finally found out. All our friends know. I'm the last to find out. Why are lovers always the last to know?"

"I don't know."

"Anyway, who cares?" She held out her hand. "Come here, Alex." I paused for a moment. She looked so beautiful in her grief and her pain and her passion. I wanted her more than ever, and I could see that she wanted me, but for all the wrong reasons. She wanted to use me to get back at her cheating girlfriend. I could have been anybody. As for me — I'd be a homewrecker, the other woman. I'd be corrupting the morals of a married woman. I looked back at her and I knew I didn't care. She wanted me, and that's all that mattered. Ever since she had walked into Gulliver's Travel and into my life, with that gorgeous body and all her femme charm, I knew that this moment would come.

I saw her outstretched hand and I took it. She pulled me to her and I went. I raised my free hand to her beautiful, angry face and I kissed her. My passion was an ancient volcano. Lava had been building up for hundreds of years inside my aching body. My desire for her was immense. I poured every ounce of its greatness into that first kiss. It was a kiss to die for, deep and wet and explosive. She pulled away and looked at me, trying to catch her breath. I waited to see what she would do. She licked her lips provocatively. Then she flung herself back into my arms, her mouth on mine, hard and urgent and wanting. We kissed again and I wrapped my arms around her, pulling her toward me, desperate to touch her all over. I wanted to see her naked. From the beginning I'd been watching her, undressing her with my eyes, wondering how her body would feel next to mine. I pulled back from her and slowly began to undo the tiny buttons on her purple silk blouse. She rested her hands lightly on my waist and watched. The smooth material slid down her arms easily. I caught the shirt as it fell and carefully hung it on the corner of a shelf. Then I stepped back a few inches so I could see her better. Her soft round tits spilled out over the top of her black lacy bra.

"Feel them," she said. "I know you want to."

I raised my hands and held her breasts, feeling the weight of them, feeling her nipples grow hard. She reached behind and undid the clasp. The elastic loosened and her bra fell into my hands. I couldn't contain myself any longer. I moved in and buried my face in her fullness. She ran her fingers through my hair and then down my back.

"Take off your shirt," she ordered.

I pulled back again as I tore at my buttons and ripped off my shirt, letting it fall to the floor near my feet. I wrapped my arms around her waist, pulling her into me tightly. My hands were around her ass. She was half sitting on my thigh. I could feel her heat right through her skirt. She was warm and wet and ready for me. I reached for her tenderly and slipped my hands under the waistband of her panties. She spread her legs apart, and I moved my hand onto her slippery cunt. She moaned and forced herself onto my eager fingers, and then I remembered. I pulled back out. She looked up at me with big questioning eyes.

"What's wrong, Alex?"

"Shit!" I said. "God, I miss the seventies."

"What?!"

"Safe sex. You know. We need latex gloves or a dental dam, a condom, anything."

"Oh, god." Her desire for me was palpable. There had to be something we could do. I pulled free of her and looked around, leaving her leaning against the shelves, out of breath and longing. I staggered into the lunchroom, searching for something, anything that even resembled a latex glove. Desperately, I looked in the fridge. The answer was staring me in the face. On the bottom rack my uneaten cheese sandwich from the day before still sat in a clear plastic bag. I laughed and lunged for it. The sandwich slipped out and I tossed it into the garbage. I went back to her, holding up my prize, and she giggled as I shook out the crumbs and slid my hand into the baggie.

"Oh, Alex, don't make me wait any longer," she hissed, and I was back in her arms, my gloved hand up her dress and inside her underwear. Urgently I felt for her opening and slid one finger in. She grabbed for me with her cunt and I gave her another finger and then another. She was moving on me like her life depended on it. In all my thirty-odd years I had never been with such a wild woman. The world slipped away from us. We were nothing but a hand and a cunt, and she tore at the flesh on my back with her nails, crying, "Yes, baby, yes, I want you to fuck me, don't stop." And I gave her all that I had to give, and she took it and took it until she was coming. Deep, heaving waves of muscles contracting on my fingers.

"Oh, Sadie. You're beautiful," I whispered in her ear, and I meant every word. I was so happy I thought I would burst.

Then I held her as her breathing calmed and she clutched me, her body tight against mine. We were sweating right onto the sheets of Xerox paper. My hand was still inside of her. I think we were in love, just for that moment. She was still my boss. She still had a lover who cheated on her. But in that instant we were the two happiest dykes the world had ever known. I wanted it to go on forever.

I knew that soon she would pull away, adjust her clothes, and we would both go home. She to her lover. I to my empty apartment. We would not fall in love. She would not leave her lover for me. She would still be my boss. And I would keep on searching for the woman of my dreams. And yet, each Monday morning, when I drag myself reluctantly into work for the start of another long week, I knew I'd always have Sadie, the beautiful voluptuous boss lady, across the room to daydream about. I'd never forget the feel of her cunt on my hand, the softness of her breasts against mine, or her powerful, womanly scent.

I reached up and stroked her hair, and we stayed like that for a long time. Then I brought my lips to hers and we kissed. I felt her body moving just a little, her passion building again. I smiled because I knew that the great romantics would always have Paris, Bogart and Bergman would always have Casablanca, and for the rest of our lives, Sadie and I would always have Gulliver's Travel.

About the contributors

✦✦✦✦

Lucy Jane Bledsoe is an ex-ranger who now writes and teaches. She is the editor of *Goddesses We Ain't: Tenderloin Women Writers* (Freedom Voices Publications, 1992). Her short fiction has appeared in *Newsday, Evergreen Chronicles, Girljock, Conditions, Focus,* and *Caprice,* and in many anthologies, including *Dykescapes* (Alyson, 1991) and *Women on Women* 2 (NAL/Dutton, 1993).

Karne Cutter is a former housecleaner who lives in the Boston area.

Dorianne Erickson Moore is a lesbian vegetarian in her late twenties living in Southern California with her cats. She loves cunts and skateboarding.

Katherine Fugate holds a B.A. in theatre arts and journalism and has been working in the entertainment industry for the past seven years. She lives in Los Angeles with her cat and her rooms of many colors, and is currently finishing her first novel. She hopes that somehow, somewhere, Anaïs Nin is very proud.

Jane Futcher is the author of *Crush* and *Promise Not to Tell*. Her erotic writing has appeared in *Bushfire: Stories of Lesbian Desire* and

The Poetry of Sex. She's a founding editor of the *Slant*, a gay, lesbian, and bisexual newspaper in Marin County, California.

Willyce Kim was the first Asian lesbian published in the United States. Between January and June she can often be found at Golden Gate Fields playing the ponies. She lives in Oakland, California, with Campbell, Blue, and Meepie. She is the author of two works of fiction, *Dancer Dawkins and the California Kid* and *Dead Heat*, both published by Alyson.

Mia Levesque is a 27-year-old writer living in Philadelphia. She shares her apartment with Sophie the rabbit and, quite often, with Dillan the dog. "Emilee Begins to Learn" is her first story.

Pam McArthur is a writer living in eastern Massachusetts with her life partner, Beth, and their son, Aaron. She thanks Beth and the terrific women of her writers' group; without them, her writing would probably still be hidden away on her closet shelf. Her work has appeared in *Common Lives/Lesbian Lives*, *Backspace*, and the anthologies *Shattered Silences* and *Bushfire: Stories of Lesbian Desire*.

Alice McCracken, Ph.D., single-parented an adopted child and spent fifteen years as a psychotherapist in Arizona before concluding that something important was missing from her life. Walking out on her private practice at the age of forty-seven, she moved to San Diego, where she took up sailing, metaphysics, and creative writing — and came out of the closet. Alice has been a lifelong movie buff and for the past two years has worked as an assistant manager in a movie theater. At one time a journalist, she has recently published several personal-experience articles; "Cinema Scope" marks her debut as a fiction writer.

Debra Moskowitz has spent her last fifteen years focused on traveling, growing, writing, and enjoying herself, with the love of her life and sometime collaborator, the painter Elin Menzies. They have published a children's book about a baby bat's first flight called

Taking Katy for a Nightride. Debra is happy that her inclusion in this anthology semilegitimizes the time she's dedicated to sexual fantasy (or at least some portion of it).

Cynthia Perry is a professor of literature and the author of numerous scholarly articles that few people have ever bothered to read. In recent years, she has turned to more interesting kinds of writing, such as the story included in this collection. She hopes eventually to make enough money from creative writing to retire from academic life and devote herself to her cats, her dog, her garden, and her charming companion, Lucie.

Nice Rodriguez was born and raised in the Philippines. She came to Canada in 1988 and presently lives and works in Toronto. Her first collection of short stories, *Throw It to the River,* will be published in the fall of 1993 by Women's Press.

Patricia Roth Schwartz lives on Weeping Willow Farm in central New York, where she grows organic produce, herbs, and Christmas trees. She is also a college teacher, a psychotherapist, and an herbalist. Her collection of humor and an anthology of lesbian erotica she is editing will be out in 1994 from New Victoria.

Chris Strickling is a free-lance writer living in Austin, Texas. She has a small private practice in occupational therapy and is pursuing a Ph.D. in English and women's studies. Writing is what keeps her sane while doing the work of being a single mother, going to school, and trying to make a living.

Jean Swallow is a lesbian-feminist writer and editor who has lived in the San Francisco Bay Area for the last thirteen years, while her books *Out from Under: Sober Dykes and Our Friends* and *Leave a Light On for Me* were published. She currently has her house on the market and is planning to move to Seattle as soon as it is sold.

Karen X. Tulchinsky is a Jewish lesbian political activist writer who lives in Vancouver, Canada, with her lover, Suzanne. Her fiction has appeared in several anthologies including *Getting Wet* (Women's

Press) and *Lovers* (Crossing Press). She has stories forthcoming in *Sister/Stranger* (Sidewalk Revolution Press) and *Love's Shadow* (Crossing Press).

Susan Wade, an Atlanta native, writes of her experiences and fantasies as a dyke out twenty-five years. She tries to capture in her works the philosophy that lesbian sex, above all, should be lots of fun. She is currently completing *The Lesbian's Bedside Reader and Coloring Book,* a collection of her erotic writings and line drawings, from which "Telefon" is taken.

Other books of interest from
ALYSON PUBLICATIONS

BUSHFIRE, edited by Karen Barber, $9.00. Amidst our differences, all lesbians share one thing: a desire for women. Sometimes intensely sexual, other times subtly romantic, this emotion is always incredibly powerful. These short stories celebrate lesbian desire in all its forms.

THE LESBIAN SEX BOOK, by Wendy Caster, $15.00. Covering topics from age differences to vibrators, anonymous sex to vegetables, this illustrated handbook is perfect for newly out lesbians as well as those who want to discover more about lesbian sexuality.

CHOICES, by Nancy Toder, $9.00. In this straightforward, sensitive novel, Nancy Toder conveys the joys — and fears — of a woman coming to terms with her attraction to other women.

DAUGHTERS OF THE GREAT STAR, by Diana Rivers, $10.00. The daughters of the Great Star, all born in the same year, soon found themselves estranged from their villages and even from their families. But they found one another, and created their own world of strong and sensual women.

THE FIRST GAY POPE, by Lynne Yamaguchi Fletcher, $8.00. The first gay pope, the earliest lesbian novel, the biggest gay bookstore, and the worst anti-gay laws, are all recorded in this entertaining new reference book.

LEAVE A LIGHT ON FOR ME, by Jean Swallow, $10.00. Real life in real time for four San Francisco lesbians: cold coffee in the kitchen, hot sex on the side, with friendships strong enough to pull them all through.

MACHO SLUTS, by Pat Califia, $10.00. Pat Califia has put together a stunning collection of her best erotic short fiction. She explores sexual fantasy and adventure in previously taboo territory.

MELTING POINT, by Pat Califia, $10.00. The author of the best-selling *Macho Sluts* returns with an all-new collection of erotica that scorches the page.

ONE TEENAGER IN TEN, edited by Ann Heron, $5.00. One teenager in ten is gay. Here, twenty-six young people from around the country discuss their coming-out experiences. Their words will provide encouragement for other teenagers facing similar experiences.

THE PERSISTENT DESIRE, edited by Joan Nestle, $15.00. Through personal essays, short fiction, poetry, interviews, and photographs, some eighty women explore femme and butch identities in the lesbian community.

UNBROKEN TIES, by Carol S. Becker, $10.00. Through a series of personal accounts and interviews, Dr. Carol Becker, a practicing psychotherapist, charts the various stages of lesbian break-ups and examines the ways women maintain relationships with their ex-lovers.

THE ALYSON ALMANAC, by Alyson Publications, $9.00. The Alyson Almanac is the most complete reference book available about the lesbian and gay community — and also the most entertaining. Here are brief biographies of some 300 individuals from throughout history; a report card for every member of congress; significant dates from our history; addresses and phone numbers for major organizations, bookstores, periodicals, and hotlines; and much more.

BI ANY OTHER NAME, edited by Loraine Hutchins and Lani Kaahumanu, $12.00. In this ground-breaking anthology, over seventy women and men from all walks of life describe their lives as bisexuals in prose, poetry, art, and essays.

THE WANDERGROUND, by Sally Miller Gearhart, $9.00. Gearhart's stories imaginatively portray a future women's culture, combining a control of mind and matter with with a sensuous adherence to their own realities.

TRAVELS WITH DIANA HUNTER, by Regine Sands, $8.00. When 18-year-old Diana Hunter runs away from her hometown of Lubbock, Texas, she begins an unparalleled odyssey of love, lust, and humor that spans almost twenty years.

BEHIND THE MASK, by Kim Larabee, $7.00. In this lesbian regency romance, a nineteenth-century English woman feels stifled by her upper-class milieu, and escapes by leading a double life as a highway robber.

SUPPORT YOUR LOCAL BOOKSTORE

Most of the books described here are available at your nearest gay or feminist bookstore, and many of them will be available at other bookstores. If you can't get these books locally, order by mail using this form.

Enclosed is $_____ for the following books. (Add $1.00 postage if ordering just one book. If you order two or more, we'll pay the postage.)

1._____

2._____

3._____

name:_____

address:_____

city:_____state:_____zip:_____

ALYSON PUBLICATIONS
Dept. J-51, 40 Plympton St., Boston, MA 02118

After December 31, 1994, please write for current catalog.